THE WEE MEN
OF BALLYWOODEN

"Well, well," said Danny O'Fay, "where did you come from?"

THE WEE MEN
OF BALLYWOODEN

BY

ARTHUR MASON

WITH ILLVSTRATIONS
BY ROBERT LAWSON

COACHWHIP PUBLICATIONS
GREENVILLE, OHIO

TO

THE WEE MEN,

FRIENDS OF MY

CHILDHOOD

The Wee Men of Ballywooden, by Arthur Mason
Illustrated by Robert Lawson
© 2026 Coachwhip Publications edition

First published 1930
Arthur Mason, 1876-1955
CoachwhipBooks.com

ISBN 1-61646-629-4
ISBN-13 978-1-61646-629-9

CONTENTS

ILLUSTRATIONS

THE NIGHT
OF THE
BIG WIND

CHAPTER ONE

OLD DANNY O'FAY and his donkey lived in a hut
by the sea, and Danny sold fish through the
country. People wondered how he got his fish. He
was never known to buy from fishermen, nor did he
ever fish himself. But before he went to bed, he put
the wee saddle on his donkey. Another thing he did,
and he never missed a night. He would fill his clay
pipe, and light it and puff on it for a bit. Then he'd

open the door and lay the smoking pipe on the door-step, saying as he yawned, "A fine night it is, with the sea talking and the corncrake singing. Well, have your smoke and take your donkey ride. You'll not be forgetting my fish for the morning. Good-night to yez all." Then he'd close and bar the door and lie down on his bed of straw and sleep until Jerry, his donkey, hee-hawed him awake. Then up he'd get and open the door and out to his two-wheel cart he'd go, to look at his fish. There they'd be, fresh from the sea, every one of them. Old Danny would smile the gouged wrinkles from his face. "Ah, and it's the fine catch they had last night," he'd say.

This had been going on for quite a while, and old Danny and his donkey thrived fairly well. He had his bowl of red tea, and potatoes and cabbage, and once in a while the leg of a duck. Old Danny was happy as he drove through the country shouting his song, "Fresh fish! Fresh fish! Fresh fish!"

Then came a day when old Danny's customers questioned his honesty.

"Say, Danny O'Fay," they asked, "where do you get your fish? You never buy from fishermen, nor do you ever fish yourself."

4

"Is it stealing fish you're thinking I am?"

"Oh, the Lord forbid," said Mrs. Blaney, "and us eating every morsel of them! It isn't that at all, at all, Danny O'Fay, but worse. Our eyes we've been keeping on you lately, and it's said by word of mouth, that in the dark of the moon, wee lights are seen dancing around your hut. Now, Danny O'Fay, if it's harboring Willie the Wisp you are, and all of his clan, not a fish will we buy from you."

"Tut, tut," said Danny, "you're all astray in your mind. It's eating too much oatmeal you are, and not enough fish out of the sea."

"Away with you, Danny O'Fay," they scolded. "Look at the saddle marks on your donkey! How do you explain that?"

"I do a bit of riding in my sleep," answered Danny. "And as for the wee lights you do be seeing in the dark of the moon, sure it may be the flicker of your own candle lights that you haven't blinked out of your eyes."

"Oh, no, Danny O'Fay, it's pious men have seen the lights, and they have warned us to buy no more of your fish. Away with you, now!"

"Get up!" said Danny to his donkey. "It's terrible

times we do be having, with people not believing, nor buying my fish. Well, well, what will become of us anyway?"

All day long he drove through the country but not a fish could he sell. Nor would the farmers speak to him when he passed. They looked the other way. So, heartsore and weary, he turned his donkey homeward, and by the time he reached the four roads, a mile or more from his hut, a wall of clouds banked the setting sun.

Old Danny looked up at the cloud-growing sky. Said he to himself, "I hear the crows scolding on the wing to their nests, but not a sight of one do I see. Put longer strides into your steps!" he shouted to his donkey. "Is it blind you are, that you can't see the clouds falling? Don't be listening to the frogs croaking or the crickets a-singing. Can't you hear the wind starting a fight in the whins? On with you, I say, before the pitch of the night swallows us up!" And Danny trudged on behind his donkey cart, thinking the while of the wind, and the power of it, and of the morrow with the fish in his cart left to rot.

The road now ribboned itself along the strand, and Danny looked out at the sea. "The Wee Men will be doing no fishing to-night," said he to himself, "not with the waves coughing the hearts out of themselves the way they are. Ah, and sure I'll have to be telling them to put their wee nets away. I can't sell a fish. There's a blight upon me. But they'll have their smoke and their donkey ride just the same."

Night came in like a crow lighting on a nest of eggs. Danny was home, unhitching his donkey.

"Ah, what a night! What a night!" he was saying. But he couldn't hear himself talk, for the wind stole the words out of his mouth as fast as his tongue could twist them. "Ah, there'll be a world of trouble to-night. I, with my five and seventy winters, have never listened to the lung-moanings of the wind like this before." He fumbled for the buckle on the donkey's collar. "Keep your ears away from my hands, bad cess to you, and me trying to get you out of the wind."

He opened the door of his hut. There was a wee turf fire burning in the grate. "Good-evening to yez all," he said. "My eyes don't see one of you, but sure that's nothing at all, with a night of nights outside. Come in, Jerry," he said to the donkey, "and be thankful you have a roof over your head." At that moment, the wind lifted a blanket of thatch off the roof. "I may have spoken a bit too quick; anyway, there's a fire in the grate, and your stall is over yonder."

Danny closed and barred the door. The wind tumbled through the hole in the roof and filled the hut. He tried to light a candle but the wind wouldn't let him. He pulled off his cap, scratched a wisp of hair over his ear, and looked up at the roof.

"Where's the moon to-night? Bad luck to her, the hag that she is. You never can see her when you want her. Oh, it's not angry I am at all. It's feeding the donkey I'll be doing." He felt his way to the stall. There stood the donkey eating oats. "What!" exclaimed old Danny. "Did they feed you before they left? Well, well, God bless every one of them! May the roots of the trees take a good grip of the ground while the Wee Men hold onto them, for it's something firm they'll be needing to-night. Ah, why don't they have houses like human beings? But it's not for me to tamper with things that are and things that are not. Anyway, they'll have their smoke, even if the wind lifts the world on its wings."

Danny sat down by the fire and filled his pipe and

8

lit it. He smoked for a bit, then he got up and opened the door to lay his pipe down on the doorstep. The storm, like a byre full of bullocks chased by bumble-bees, knocked the pipe out of his hand, and the mouth of the wind gulped its sparks.

"You gluttonous villain!" shouted old Danny. "May the sparks burn a hole in your thrapple!" He placed his back against the door and with his sharp shoulder blades he closed it. "Sure," said he, "it feels as if the tops of the mountains were playing hop, skip, and jump. Oh, what a night for my wee friends to be out in. No shelter, no smoke, and the world rolling under them."

As old Danny hobbled over to the fire the only window in the hut blew in and crashed around his feet. A roar ran up the chimney and the wee fire chased after it. And to make matters worse, the thatched roof was stripped entirely. Danny was blown against the door, and he stood there, rubbing his hands.

"Is it afraid I am?" he cried. "Tut, tut, Danny O'Fay, put that thought out of your head. It's not the wind you're listening to, at all. It's the music from the big tumbling waves you're hearing." He got down on his hands and knees, and crawled to the donkey stall. "Get over there, Jerry. It's Danny that's talking. Don't you hear me? Get over, I say. Shake the roar out of your ears. There isn't an eye-cup of sleep in the world to-night, but it's lying alongside of you I'll be doing. If the wild mane of the blow leaves the walls standing, we'll both be here in the morning. Whist! Is that whispering I'm hearing, or is it the wind counting the spokes in the wheels of my cart?"

Old Danny lay down under the manger, talking to himself, and closed his eyes.

CHAPTER TWO

THE PAVER OF CAVES

THE Big Wind wrought havoc through the country that night. Nothing escaped. Cattle sheds were up-ended. Chimneys tumbled down. Sheets of bog water went flying through the air. The four roads were choked with haystack tops and jaunting cars. Thorns and whin bushes were plucked out by the roots. Hedgehogs, wheelbarrows—all sorts of things were loose and on the run.

13

THE WEE MEN OF BALLYWOODEN

Blaney's rooster, that weighed a stone and could crow louder than any rooster in the parish, got stuck in the garden gate. The wind nibbled him naked. The old windmill on Murry's Brae, that hadn't run for years, was spinning to-night, and the squeaks from it sounded louder than a drove of hungry pigs.

The oak tree in the lonely lane had been the talk of generations. It was whispered in the ears of young and old that the Wee Men spent some of their nights in the lonely lane and played around the oak tree.

THE NIGHT OF THE BIG WIND

And there wasn't a man in the parish who would pass it after dark. Anyway, the wind hurled against it and it came crashing to the ground. There was no shelter anywhere. The cow paths looked twisted, and the stepping stiles were open gaps. Even the rushes in the meadow lay like combed hair.

Down by the sea, where a mossy rock lipped over a cove, swarms of Wee Men were hanging, clinging to the moss. The chief of the clan—the Paver-of-Caves —was renowned among the Wee Men for his ability

to blend moonflakes with white heather for the flooring of the caves. To-night he was so fearfully frightened that he could hardly make himself heard, even though he spoke in his loudest voice.

"I hope the moss on this rock holds," he cried. "Were there any of you scratched when the oak tree fell?"

"No, no," came wee whines, "but we're all warped and twisted. Our eyes are webbed with eyebrows, and our beards are whistling tunes such as we never heard before!"

"That's to be expected," answered the Paver. "Keep your heads! Don't let the belching waves or the sky wheezings upset you. If the moss holds, well and good. If it doesn't, keep together, whatever happens!"

A wee wail of a voice reached the Paver's ears. "The moss on this rock is as straggly as the down on a young linnet's breast!"

"Who is that I hear?" asked the Paver.

"The Midsummer Mower," came back the answer.

"I thought as much," cried the Paver. "You're always complaining of a poor harvest. Now then, weigh down your minds," commanded the Paver. "Weigh

them down well, with the work you've left undone—
and trust to that to hold you to the rock!"

The Wee Men had no difficulty weighing down
their minds, but even that weight was no match for
the night. All of a sudden, without the yelp of a
warning, the arms of the wind began wrestling with
the rock.

"Let go," roared the Paver, "before we're tossed
into the cove! There's slugging behind us, but no-
wheres ahead of us. Unballast your minds! Take hold
of each other!"

A buzzing of wee voices hummed through the
blackness.

"Oh, where are we going?"

"That," shouted the Paver, "is a question I can't
answer."

The words were no sooner out of his mouth than
the tail of the wind wound itself around the Wee Men
and lifted them high in the air.

"We're all right, so far!" the Paver cried out. "Stick
together! Don't let go of each other! If I had an eye-
ful of moonlight I could tell you which way we're
going."

"The sea is under us!" screamed the Crane Chaser.

The Midsummer Mower, who had hold of the Paver's hand, cried out in a tremble, "Have you no power at all?"

"Power?" shrieked back the Paver. "With my feet off the ground? Why, man, what are you thinking about? Power? I'd have you all know that, with the stars mired, and the moon choked, I can do nothing but blow away with the rest of you."

The gale was sweeping them out over the sea. The wee Cradle Rocker began to cry. "I'm getting dizzy from whirling and circling," he whined.

"Stop your crying!" commanded the Paver. "There's noise enough in the world to-night."

"If only I had a light," called out the Cradle Rocker, "I could find myself."

"Hold on," shouted the Paver, "there may be a remedy after all. Is Willie the Wisp among you?"

"That I am," piped up Willie, "but I haven't a spare breath to blow my light lit."

"Where do you think we are now?" spoke the Stooker-of-Wheat-Sheaves.

Grunty, the fisherman, answered, "Over Dundrum Bay."

"We're all right, so far!" the Paver cried out.

THE NIGHT OF THE BIG WIND

"If the clouds should let go of us," shouted the Wee Weaver, "I won't have to do any more weaving!"

"Stop your complaining," ordered the Paver. "I'll need a suit the minute we alight."

"How about me?" It was the Quarryman's voice. "My schisty shirt is slit up the back. My cap is gone and my pulse heaters, too. How are we going to get back? Can you answer me that, Paver-of-Caves?"

"We're speeding so fast," answered the Paver, "that my mind can't keep up with me."

There was silence among the Wee Men for a long time, for they had little breath to waste in words. They held tight to each other's hands, while the Big Wind made serpentine curves out of them, as on it swept over the sea, driving them ahead of it. But after a while the Counter-of-Lark-Eggs spoke. Said he, "I smell the morn, and it's fighting its way to be seen."

"Good," said the Paver, "I thought we were near-ing something, for I just bumped my chilblain on the top of a mountain."

Far, far away, the tired eye of the morn squeezed through the clouds. Ribbons of sunken sunlight fluttered up and into the sky. And then something happened that brought cheer to the Wee Men, for all of a sudden they found themselves astride the arch of a rainbow.

"Let go of hands," commanded the Paver, "and every man of you slide down the rainbow legs to the ground! But mind and keep your heads, for we don't know what's waiting below."

The Wee Men began to argue about what colors they would choose to slide down.

"Look here," said the Paver, "there are colors enough for all of you. I'm going down on the peacock band."

"I'll follow you on the purple," said the Weaver. "I might even do a bit of weaving on my way down."

"Good!" cried the Paver. "I'm in need of a cloak. Have an eye out for color; it's a green cloak I want."

The Paver looked over his men. "Are you all ready?" he asked.

"We are!"

"Then let us slide down to the ground!"

The Wee Men lay flat on their little bellies, and

each one twisted his short legs around the color band he liked best. Then down the rainbow legs they banistered.

The Weaver was the last to land, for he had a large bundle of woven rainbow web under his arm.

CHAPTER THREE

THE Paver gathered his men around him. Said
he, "One thing is certain. The sky wheezings are
sleeping down here. We're in a country of tall trees,
where there's nothing but shadows. And what could
be worse? There may be strange things in this forest
of trees—people we know nothing about. We'll have
to be careful, if we wander around, and not get familiar with mortals."

29

THE WEE MEN OF BALLYWOODEN

The Mower sat down with his back against a tree. "Come what may," he said, "I have got to talk. Here we are and here we're nowhere. Where's the country we left behind? That's what I want to know." He looked at the Paver.

The chief of the clan was showing the effects of the night. His nose was listed from the ramming of it by the Big Wind, and his ears wobbled. His boots and brier-leaf stockings were missing, and Fear had dug wee ditches in his face.

"For one thing," went on the Mower, "before we think much of anything else, we must have clothes, and have them at once."

"Silence!" commanded the Paver. "I can see myself having trouble with you. I'm not in the mood this morning to listen to whines. You're a terrible sight, all of you, but I couldn't help our being blown away. I must think out a way back."

Grunty the Fisherman yawned. Said he, "I'm not complaining, but I'm thinking a bit. I'm thinking of old Danny O'Fay. It's a smoke from his pipe I'd like just now."

The Paver hiccoughed. "Get that smoke out of

your head," he said. "We've other things to think about."

"I should say we have," put in the Cradle Rocker. "Who will be rocking Delaney's sick baby, with me away, and not knowing where I am?" He looked at the Paver, the chief of the clan. "Do you know where we are?"

"I don't," said the Paver, "but my wits may be here any minute."

The Midsummer Mower interrupted. "You'll be needing more than wits to get us back again. Where's your power, anyway? I'm not saying you haven't got any."

"You'd better not," snapped the Paver. "Who brought on the rainbow for you this morning? You should be thankful you're down on the ground. Here, we're somewhere, but in the clouds we were nowhere."

The Quarryman jumped to his feet. "Whist!" he cried. "There's hammering in my head. I'm drilling an idea. I was not without power, myself, in days gone by. I could milk a goat, and count the scales on a shad."

"Oh, I can remember that time," said the Stooker-of-Wheat-Sheaves.

"Silence!" ordered the Paver. "Let the Quarryman go on with his drilling."

Then all were silent, and after a while the Quarryman spoke. "I have it! We'll tunnel a way home."

"Sit down!" commanded the Paver. "Your brain is tweedling, and as for your drillings, they are just as I thought—holes that would lead to nowhere. While we're here we'll make the best of it."

The Mower scratched his wee spine, that wasn't any longer than the shank of old Danny's pipe. He looked at the Paver. "You're not speaking for me when you talk about making the best of anything here," said he. "I'm going back, if I have to mow a swath around the world."

The Paver's ears grew red with anger. "If I hear another word from you, I'll turn you into a cricket."

"You haven't the power," answered the Mower. "If you'd had the least bit of power, you'd have stopped the sky wheezings, and we wouldn't be here."

The Paver's eyes began to bulge. He jumped to his feet.

THE NIGHT OF THE BIG WIND

"Look out!" cried the Cradle Rocker. "If you're changed into a cricket, you'll be no help at all."

The Paver sprang toward the Mower, uttering strange words, but just at that moment, a shaft of young sunlight struck the Paver and down he fell. He wiggled himself into the shadow, and when he got his breath again he looked around him. Said he, "Are we all here?"

"Oh, to be sure," answered the Stooker. "We haven't moved a hair."

"I wasn't expecting that blow from the sun," said the Paver, "but being in a strange country, I suppose I didn't make a safe allowance for distance. Anyway," he looked at the Mower, "let this be a warning to you. For the time being I'll leave you as you are, but if I hear any more blathering out of you, either as to how we got here or how we get back, the sun's jolts won't save you. And this means all of you. I'm the chief of this clan, and what I say goes."

The Counter-of-Lark-Eggs asked if he might speak.

"You may," answered the Paver.

"We're all out of sorts," said the Counter, "but we're not a bad little band. We'll get back to the land where my larks sing, and we'll hear Blaney's rooster crow again. And the Mower shall mow the mists off the meadows, and the Stooker shall stook his wheat sheaves, too. Yes, and the Cradle Rocker shall hush the farmers' wee babies."

Tears began to dribble from out the Paver's eyes. Said he, "You've forgotten all about the caves, and the time I've spent tamping moonflakes and white heather."

"You have missed me, too!" piped up the Crane Chaser. "But I'll tell you one thing: if I could screech an echo, I might tell you where we are."

"Silence!" ordered the Paver. "You're getting things mixed. The Counter-of-Lark-Eggs has put the heart back into me," he went on. "Now for business. How many of you are without boots? Put up your hands. What! Have all your boots blown away?"

"I still have mine," shouted Willie the Wisp.

"And how happens that?" asked the Paver.

"Well," said Willie, "that's simple enough. I tied them fast to the warts on my knees."

"Good," said the Paver, "I might give you all warts to tie yourselves to." Then the Paver turned to the Weaver. "Did you weave enough of a web out of the rainbow leg to make cloaks for all of the Wee Men?" he asked.

"I did," said the Weaver, "for I looked over the clan before we came down and saw what would be needed."

"Get cloaks on them, then," commanded the Paver. "And remember, men, no arguing about colors. There's a green one for me, and that settles that."

The Midsummer Mower took courage and spoke. "It's a straw colored cloak that I'll be wearing!"

The Paver stared at him, and the Mower's mouth closed.

In no time at all the Weaver had fitted each man with a cloak. The last piece of web was all green, and that the Weaver hung over the shoulders of the Paver.

Then Grunty the Fisherman called for boots. "It's boots we must have, for there are thistles about. We're bound to get scared in these strange woods, and we may have to do some running."

"Hold on," said the Paver, "I'm thinking a bit. I may have lost the receipt for the boots. Silence, all of you. No blowing of noses, or coughing or sneezing, till the lost receipt comes into my thinking."

THE WEE MEN OF BALLYWOODEN

The wee barefooted men stood huddled together. Not a thought did they think nor an eye did they wink, for the matter of boots was a serious thing. Then all of a sudden the Paver lay down with his ear to the ground, and listened.

The Mower whispered to the Counter-of-Lark-Eggs, "The Paver acts as if he had colic."

"Whist!" warned the Counter. "Don't confuse thoughts with him now."

Pretty soon, up jumped the Paver, pursing his lips. He threw back his head and whistled. Whatever he was whistling for, took a long time coming.

A smile came into the Mower's face. He nudged the Counter—"The Paver is powerless," said he.

At that moment the Paver stopped whistling. A woolly look came into his eyes. "Men," he said, "you can see for yourselves. I'm too far away to whistle for boots."

"I knew your power was pulverless," spoke up the Mower. "I knew it last night when the oak tree fell."

The Paver squared his wee shoulders and settled his eyes on the Mower. "Something tells me," said he, "you are wishful of trouble. It's not through lack of my power that you are no cricket right now. Remem-

36

ber, it's not so long ago that you were a field mouse, carrying wisps of straw to the red fox den. One would think, to hear you blathering, that it was all my fault because the sky wheezings wheezed us here. Now, if I hear another word out of you, I may change you into something that I won't be disposed to change again."

A shadow silence fell upon them, while the Wee Men looked at one another and wondered. The Paver broke the silence.

"Is the Meadow Sniffer here?"

A Wee Man, with a wilted daisy look about his face, answered, "Yes."

"Come here, then; I have something to say to you." The Paver whispered softly in his ear, "Do you know a receipt for boots? It looks as if my power hasn't caught up with me yet. But it will come—it will come—and when it does, the Mower will be the first to know about it."

"Well," said the Meadow Sniffer, "boots are entirely out of my line, but since you are hard put to provide soles for our feet, I might do some scenting. By the way, have you looked over your head yet? I mean at those tree mushrooms. They're lug-eared

37

and leathery. They'll make clogs for the clan."

"Good," said the Paver. "I see all sizes up there. But," he went on, "one thing we're forgetting, and that is how we're to fasten them onto our feet."

The Meadow Sniffer sniffed. "How about threading them onto our feet with spider webs?"

"No," cried the Paver, "we'll make insoles of the cobwebs. They'll hold the mushroom clogs to our feet."

The Paver then swallowed a mouthful of air to give him lung power to command. He puffed out his chest. "Men," he shouted, "climb that tree, and measure your feet for mushroom clogs! When you're satisfied as to size, each one of you hunt for a spider's web and insole your clogs. Then stick them to your feet, so that we can mush along and away from here before the shadows shorten."

"But where to?" whined the Cradle Rocker.

"I'm lost. We all are," snapped the Paver. "Climb that tree and shake me down a pair of clogs."

It took no time at all from the forest of time for the Wee Men to shoe themselves with mushroom clogs. Then off they set—to find out where they might be and what sort of a country they'd been blown to.

CHAPTER FOUR

THE MIDSUMMER MOWER

THE Paver and the Sniffer took the lead. Willie the Wisp and the Quarryman followed. Then came the Mower and the Cradle Rocker, and next the Stooker-of-Wheat-Sheaves and the Counter-of-Lark-Eggs. The lesser Wee Men were in the middle. Grunty the Fisherman and the Weaver had their orders to mush along behind the clan, and pick up any of the Wee Men who stumbled in their clogs.

THE WEE MEN OF BALLYWOODEN

The morning was well advanced. The sun was half high of the tallest trees, and the tree shadows were shortening, as the Paver gave his orders.

"Men, we don't know where we're going, but we'll follow the Meadow Sniffer. Remember, keep in the shadows or the sun may eat holes in your rainbow cloaks. And another thing, no dancing or jigging in your mushroom clogs. If we should meet Fear in the forest—well—you know my power. Your cloaks and clogs are proof of that."

The Weaver nudged the Fisherman. "What's that he says about cloaks?"

"He's just talking," answered Grunty. "Don't get into an argument with him now."

"March!" shouted the Paver, and the Wee Men, like a river of colored butterflies, streamed away through the green forest.

They had mushed along but a wee mile when the Mower began to grumble. He called to the Paver. "Say, are we getting anywhere, or is it just trees, trees, trees? I'm hungry, and these clogs hurt my feet. My insoles are slipping, my ankles are turning, and my tongue is as dry as a midsummer's well."

The Paver gave his green rainbow cloak a flip, and

looked back over his shoulder. Just as he did, somewhere ahead a dog barked. The Paver stopped and
held up his hand for all to halt. There were strange
squeakings in his wee voice.

"Men," he said, "the Mower's loud mouth has
brought this upon us. He has flat feet, fit for neither
clog nor boot. But enough of him. There's danger
ahead. Stop your shivering. Shivers will never get us
back to our own native land, with her sods and her
bogs, and her caves and her thorns."

The Counter-of-Lark-Eggs began to cry. "You're
forgetting the larks and the linnets, the cuckoos and
blackbirds," he wailed.

"Stop crying, all of you!" commanded the Paver.
"Don't you hear the dog barking?"

"He's coming this way," cried the Meadow Sniffer.

The Paver's knees wiggled. "He's coming this way,
did you say?"

"I can sniff his hot breath."

"Let us run!" screamed the Crane Chaser.

The Mower spoke up. "What! Run from a dog?
Not me, in these mushroom clogs."

The Paver stabbed the Mower with a stare. "I've
always thought well of you," said he. "You are good

43

at mowing lanes through morning mists. But now comes the test of your mutinous mouth. Run ahead, I command you, and meet the dog. If he's color blind, well and good, but if he's not, I'll have one man less to look after."

A murmur of dismay came from the Wee Men. To their amazement the Mower obeyed the command of the Paver. He mushed away from the clan without a look around, and was soon out of sight. The Wee Men held their breath, and the Paver cupped his ears to listen. Pretty soon there sounded a most terrifying barking and yelping. The Paver's head dropped on his chest.

Said he, "That'll be the last of the Mower for a while. He was getting unbearable, anyway."

The Cradle Rocker began to rock himself, and words slithered out of him. "I liked the Mower. The mist around cradles, he has mown for me; nor was he against rocking the farmers' sick babies."

The Paver held up his hand. "No more of that crooning. Whatever I do is best for the clan. My power is slow in coming, but it'll come sooner or later, and when it does, things will be different." He gave a tug to the Meadow Sniffer's beard. "What are you sniffing now?" he asked.

"Dog silence," replied the Sniffer.

"I thought so. It will take a slice of time to dispose of the Mower."

The wee Quarryman cleared his throat. Said he, "The Mower's calf muscles will be hard to crack. We all know that when he's in the mood, he can carry a bigger bundle of moonflakes than any man of the clan. And when it comes to mowing morning mist, his swath is wide: two men can walk it abreast."

The Counter-of-Lark-Eggs interrupted. "I have a good word for the Mower, too," said he. "He'd always leave a funnel of fog over a lark's nest, and when it came to shunting daylight out of the caves, you could always rely on the Midsummer Mower."

The Crane Chaser stared at the Paver. "May I have a word?" he asked.

The Paver nodded.

"My job is to chase wading cranes, and that keeps me limber, and I can run; you all know that. But the Mower, when he wants to, is the swiftest man of the clan."

Willie the Wisp scratched the warts on his knees

and straightened up, saying, "When the moon gets choked and won't shake flakes, it is then that my work begins. Many a night, on the rim of a hill, I, with my light, hunt for lost things. It may be a goat that has strayed far away, or a young thrush that's fallen out of its nest. But when there's a doubt in my mind, of things I can't find, I always call on the Mower."

Grunty the Fisherman wiped his eyes. "You all know my work," he said. "The job is wet and scaly. Once in a while a crab crawls into my net. It is then that I whistle for the Mower."

The Stooker-of-Wheat-Sheaves was a quiet little man. He always coughed before he spoke. "In the fields, on harvest nights," said he, "I gather stray heads of wheat, and when there's enough for sheaves I stook them. Many's the time the Mower would come. 'Here,' he'd say, 'have a puff from old Danny's clay pipe.' But now he's gone, and the harvest fields too, and so is old Danny's clay pipe."

The Wee Men began to cry, and the Paver swallowed sad lumps without tears.

The Meadow Sniffer, who was used to showering tears on wilted flowers, spilled a wee drop on his rainbow cloak, then dried his eyes and spoke. "We'd better be moving," he said to the Paver, "or grass may grow under our mushroom clogs."

The Paver raised his head and gave a command. "Every man of you shake the tears from your eyes! The Mower is gone, we all know that, but he's not worth a wail from one of you. Straighten your spines; get ready to march! Are you ready?"

"We are!"

"Then we're off!"

On, through the thick forest they mushed again. Their only guide was the sniff of the Meadow Sniffer's nose. The Paver marched with jerking eyes. He was in the lead, and somewhere ahead was a loose dog that had probably swallowed the Mower. This was the front thought in the Paver's head as he took hold of the Sniffer's hand. Said he, "I don't know what ails me. My insoles are itching the soles off my feet, and the hair on my head doesn't sway with my stride."

"I'm not myself, either," answered the Sniffer. "My eyes are tuned to color, but I don't see any here. The bracken looks shriveled, and the trunks of the trees are cold and crabbed. There's not a path nor a lane, nor the sight of a stile, nor a sniff of a haw from a hawthorne tree. If I could sniff some dew from a primrose, or hear the thrum of a bumblebee's wings——"

"No more of your bleating," snapped the Paver. "My knees are knocking together, and the pink marrow in my elbows is stiffening from listening to you."

"Whist!" hissed the Sniffer. "I sniff a waft of speed from somewhere."

"Good," cried the Paver. "As like as not, it's my power that's speeding to me."

"No," replied the Sniffer, "this is not sky speed I'm sniffing. I sniff speed that's breaking brambles."

"Well enough," said the Paver; "it might be my power after all, that's breaking its way through the tops of the trees. There's just one thing to do, and that is to catch it."

The Paver wheeled around and faced his clan. "Men," he said, "we're going to do some running. My power is adrift in this forest. Have a care for your cloaks and your mushroom clogs. Keep in the shadows. Don't let the sunlight strike you."

Then away they sped after the Sniffer's sniff of speed.

48

CHAPTER FIVE

THE Wee Men had run about the length of three steeple shadows, when the Sniffer began to sneeze.

The Paver looked pale as he puffed. "What!" he cried. "Have we come so close up to speed that you have to sneeze it?"

"I've lost the speed sniff," the Sniffer declared. "There's smoke in my sniffer."

"What!" wheezed the Paver. "Smoke in your sniffer?"

"There is, and, what's worse, there are strange humans about."

"Oh!" cried the Paver. "Don't let this rumor seep through the clan. Keep running; you may pick up the speed sniff again."

As the Wee Men skirted the edge of a bit of cleared forest, they spied a small house that had smoke coming out of its chimney, and the keen eyes of the Paver spotted near by a woodchopper carrying an ax over his shoulder and leading a child by the hand.

"Keep more in the shadow!" he called to his men.

All of a sudden, the child began to laugh.

"What are you laughing at?" the father asked her.

"Look! Look!" cried the child. "See the big butterflies!"

The father rubbed his eyes. "Tut, tut, girl," he said. "This is not the season for butterflies."

The Wee Men had disappeared into the forest again, and as they ran on, the Paver kept asking the Sniffer, "Are we running straight now?"

"We are," answered the Sniffer. "I've picked up

the speed sniff again, but I don't think it's your power we're chasing. It's far too speedy for that."

"Whatever it may be," puffed the Paver, "we'll run it down, anyway. It may lead to somewhere." Then suddenly the Paver stopped. "Halt!" he called to his men. "There's a creek here that we can neither jump nor wade."

The Wee Men were so tired after their night in the sky and the chase in the forest, that they sat down where they were and cried.

The Paver was beside himself. He didn't know what to do, so he sat down, too, and rocked his wee head in his hands.

When the Quarryman had spilled his cry, he rose to his feet and spoke to the Paver. Said he, "If the Midsummer Mower were here, he'd find a way to cross this creek."

"Yes, indeed," wailed the Cradle Rocker, "he could think, he could."

The Sniffer rolled over on his back and sniffed loudly. Then he jumped to his feet and looked down the creek. He had spied a bridge—a rainbow bridge— that crossed the creek.

The Paver let go of his head and jumped to his feet. "Men," he ordered, "get the feel of your clogs under your feet again. I knew there was a way to cross this creek."

The Sniffer led the way and examined the bridge. "It looks safe enough," said he.

"And why wouldn't it?" interrupted the Quarry-man. "I know who made this bridge."

"Who?" came a chorus of wee voices.

"The Midsummer Mower. Can't you see that's his rainbow cloak he slung across the creek?"

The Paver looked puzzled and scratched his eye-brows. "If that's the Mower's bridge, why didn't he pull it after him? And another thing, where's the dog that should have swallowed him? There are too many things for me to think about clearly." He looked at the Sniffer. "I want to know," he said, "if we have been chasing the Mower, instead of my power?"

"I'm still sniffing speed," answered the Sniffer.

The Cradle Rocker felt of the rainbow bridge with his mushroom clogs.

"Stand back there!" shouted the Paver. "I shall lead you across the rainbow bridge, one at a time. Don't get it swinging, for if it should split, likely as not, we would fall into the creek." The Paver skipped across the bridge, and each in turn followed.

The Weaver was the last to cross. Being a weaver and having an eye for material, he lifted the bridge after him and tucked it under his arm, saying as he did, "This shaving of rainbow may come in handy. I may run more lightly without it, but if we ever stop running, I'll weave the North Star into it and it may point us a course to somewhere."

"You're right," said the Paver. "You're the only Wee Man that has kept his head clear since we were blown away from our land."

While the Paver and the Weaver were talking, the Crane Chaser let a scream out of him. Every one of the Wee Men shivered with fear, for not more than a marble shot away, was a black dog coming toward them.

"Stand still, every man of you!" whispered the Paver. He nudged the Counter-of-Lark-Eggs. "Does he look as if he'd swallowed the Mower?"

"No, he's as empty as a skull, and as tired as a hunted stag."

As the dog came abreast of the Wee Men, he looked at the rainbow cloaks and growled. Not a man of them moved a clog, but their heartbeats fluttered their cloaks.

Only the Quarryman's breath came freely. He spoke that all might hear. "It's plain to be seen that dog has been chasing wee bits of rainbow. But he's not been nibbling the heels of the Midsummer Mower. Look at him!"

The Paver found his voice. "There's not a sign of the Mower's ghost in his eyes."

The dog trotted up to the creek and stopped.

The wee Quarryman laughed. "Look at him!" he went on. "There's not a jump left in him. The Mower has run all the jumps out of him."

The dog waded into the creek and lapped the water greedily. Then he wallowed across to the other side, where he stood on the bank and shook himself.

"Take your eyes away from him!" commanded the Paver. "We'll be moving on again. The shadows are lengthening, and that's a good sign."

"Are we going to do some more running?" asked the Stooker-of-Wheat-Sheaves.

"No," said the Paver, "we'll walk along till the moon comes up, and by then I may amble into my power."

"But where are we going?" cried the wee Cradle Rocker.

"We're following the Mower," answered the Sniffer.

"I don't know about that," snapped the Paver. "We've had peace since he left, and to meet up with him now will mean trouble again. The Mower knew I blew away without my power."

"We all do, for that matter," said the Quarryman, "and the worst thing that could happen has happened to me. I'm hungry."

The Cradle Rocker felt of his wee belly. "There's nothing but wrinkles inside of me. If I had a wee sip from a wee baby's bottle, I could rock the sea to sleep."

"You may have a chance," said the Paver, "for the sea we've got to cross, whether or not it is sleeping or waking, to get back to our own country."

"Isn't there a man in this clan who has a spoonful of power?" The Crane Chaser was speaking.

The Paver looked around uneasily, and then hung his head.

Grunty the Fisherman answered. "We're as free of power as I am of fish scales. I'm not complaining so much of hunger. It's a smoke I'd like, from old Danny's clay pipe. If we could but catch up with the Mower, he'd think out a way to fill us inside."

The Paver raised his head. "I've heard enough of the Mower. Silence, all of you! Put your right clogs foremost and follow the Sniffer and me."

The Wee Men obeyed and silently tottered on, while the rays from the sinking sun turned the green tops of the trees into gold. Then night wove her shadows through the forest, and Willie the Wisp lit his light as he headed the clan.

CHAPTER SIX

WILLIE THE WISP

THE Wee Men had walked well into the night before the Paver called a halt. Said he, "Men, fill
your lungs full of air and get ready for a shock. I'm
afraid that the moon, too, blew away last night. I have
no fault to find with Willie the Wisp and his wee
light, but there's not enough light to go on. My brain
is heavy and my left clog is cracked, and the string to
my wits is unraveling."

A chorus of wails came from the clan. "What! the moon blown away?"

"Alas!" said the Paver. "That's my belief."

The Weaver came up from behind and walked up to the Paver. "I've always had faith in you," he said, "but now I'm in doubt of you. Can you think of the Mower believing the moon blew away? If she was a bit lazy in waking, he'd coddle her out of her cradle. If he's somewhere among these trees to-night, he'll have his moonlight, for it's then that he does his best thinking."

The Counter-of-Lark-Eggs, who never grew ruffled, spoke up. "The moon's cradle is hinged to the stars," said he. "It may have gotten unhinged last night."

"It did," said the Paver. "I heard it squeaking, over my thinking."

"Look here," put in the Weaver, "anything that's hinged to a star stays hinged. Ever since the sea sang its first song, I've been trying to tear a patch of blue away from the stars."

"I can believe that," cried the wee Cradle Rocker. "When I rock a farmer's baby that is crying with earache, I thrust my thoughts upward to the Milky Way for a pinch of fleece."

The Quarryman interrupted. "We're full of worries, men," he said, "and it's a good thing we're full of something, or we'd still be hanging onto the rainbow legs. Now about the moon: there's no use in arguing; that'll get us nowhere. What I think about the moon is that she was jozzled last night. Suppose she is snoozing behind a crag? Let Time pry her eyes open and polish her gown. She'll sieve us our moonflakes again."

The Sniffer sneezed. The Paver nudged him. "What's the meaning of that sneeze?" said he.

"There's a smudge of light coming from somewhere," answered the Sniffer.

The Stooker-of-Wheat-Sheaves coughed. "That'll be the moon," said he, "for my right eye is twitching."

"Whist!" whispered the wee Quarryman. "Don't you hear the far-away rumble? It's the moon knocking clods off the braes as she climbs."

"It is, it is," answered the Paver. "She knows she is lagging; Time has an eye on her."

All of a sudden the moon's beams filtered through

the trees. The Paver opened his mouth wide, to give a command. Then he shut it again with a click, and stared at the clan. The moon was now pouring light on their wee swaying cloaks, and the forest of wrinkles was leaving their faces. Their bare, bushy heads were canted well forward. They were listening to a song that came from afar. The singer could be none other than the Midsummer Mower. The tune they knew well, but the words of the song they'd never heard before.

> "Oh, for my whetstone and sickle,
> And a field of morning mist!
> A lark's song, and a cuckoo's call
> From the braes of Ballywooden!"

The Weaver took hold of the Stooker and began to dance.

"Stop that!" cried the Paver. "I want to get my bearings! What's more, when I come up with the Mower, he'll hear from me. What right has he to set words to a tune without asking me?"

"Well," said the Quarryman, "the Mower's song has stirred something in me. How are we to know when the day opens its eye, without the warning crow from Blaney's big rooster?"

"That's just it," said the Paver. "The Mower and his song are filling our heads full of yesterdays. If I only had my power," and the Paver sighed, "I would sing you a song full of morrows. Anyway, we have the moon, and we can sleep on her beams. But first let us find the Mower. Follow me, men, and pay no attention to the Sniffer. When there's dew on the leaves he's sniffless."

"I can't go much farther," wailed the wee Cradle Rocker. "I'm so hungry that I think I'll lie down and eat my mushroom clogs."

"Don't you dare do that," warned the Paver. "Haven't we had bad luck enough? Some of you, I see, have been nibbling the fringe off your rainbow cloaks. We don't know where we are: we're strange to these trees, and we must keep up our spirits. If things come to the worst, I'll squander a thought, and chance on a way to feed all of you. Now, march with high heads, and show the Mower he hasn't been missed."

CHAPTER SEVEN

AHEAD of them, not a wind's whisper away, lay a wee lake surrounded by trees. Swimming about on it were a stray dozen of loons. On the bank of the lake stood an old cabin, and near by that sat the Mower, thinking into a pot.

As the clan spied him a cheer went up from the Wee Men, and they ran to greet the Mower.

"Stop!" shouted the Paver. "I'll talk to him first." He walked on ahead to the pot and the Mower. "Hello," he said. "What a sight you are! Clogless and cloakless, and mud between your toes! What's in the pot?"

"Loons' eggs," answered the Mower.

"Loons' eggs?" questioned the Paver.

"Yes, loons' eggs, and I've been waiting for Willie the Wisp to come along and kindle a fire under the pot."

"How did you know that Willie or I would come this way?" asked the Paver.

"How do I know I have eggs in the pot? Look here, Paver-of-Caves, no arguing. I had enough of that from the dog that chased me. Now he knew he was running, but what do you know? So no more of this jabber. Call the clan."

The Paver beckoned to his men. Every one of them bowed to the Mower, and then peeped into the pot. When they saw the loons' eggs they rubbed their wee empty bellies.

"Willie," said the Mower, "light the fire under the pot."

Then Willie got down on his knees with his wee torch and, in no time at all, he kindled a fire under the pot.

THE NIGHT OF THE BIG WIND

The Paver stood with folded arms eying the moon-flakes on the lake. The Mower and the Weaver were talking together. The rest of the clan sat in a circle around the pot. The Weaver pulled a rainbow cloak from under his arm. "Here," said he, "is the bridge that spanned the creek. Throw it over your shoulders again."

"Good," answered the Mower. "I thought you'd spy it, or the Sniffer would sniff it."

The Cradle Rocker spoke up. "The hunger inside me is crying, but I have never tasted a loon's egg before. I don't know whether or not to try one."

"An egg is an egg," answered the Stooker-of-Wheat-Sheaves, "wherever it is found, whether among the reeds in the bog, or in a nest in the crotch of a tree."

"I could eat anything," said the Crane Chaser. "I could even nibble the crumbs of a moonflake."

All of a sudden the loons on the lake began to cry, and such crying the Wee Men had never heard before. They jumped to their feet and started to run.

"Hold on, men," commanded the Mower. "The loons are not crying, they're singing a loon song."

The Paver's eyes blazed as he turned on the Mower.

"You have no right to command the clan. I'm the Paver-of-Caves."

The Mower faced him. "You have been the Paver-of-Caves, but to-night you're just one of us. You have no more power than the Cradle Rocker."

"Oh, don't get into an argument now," cried the Quarryman. "The moon's shadows are shortening, and the dew is weeping on the grass."

The Counter-of-Lark-Eggs spoke up. "Let us all sit down again," he said, "and be happy we're somewhere. The Paver, I know, feels fidgety."

"And why wouldn't he?" interrupted Grunty the Fisherman. "A man without power is much like a fish out of water."

"How are we to know," asked Willie the Wisp, "when the loon eggs are ready to eat?"

The Mower scanned the clan. "Is there a man among you who can answer that question?" he asked.

The Wee Men stared at the Paver, for he should be able to tell when the loon eggs were ready to eat. But there he stood with his mouth open wide, waiting for words to explain.

"Never mind," said the Mower. "His thinker is muffled. But I'll tell you when. As soon as the bubbles quit chasing each other, and the mist floats away from the top of the pot, then the loon eggs will be ready to eat."

The Cradle Rocker rubbed his wee empty belly. "But there's no sign of either bubbles or mist," he wailed.

"They will come," said the Mower, "as soon as the red fagots make coal."

The Weaver laid his hand on the Mower's shoulder. "Tell us about the dog chase, and how you found the loons' eggs," said he.

"Have a care," said the Paver, "how you listen to the Mower. He's full of himself since he potted loons' eggs, and giddy words are spilling out of him."

The Mower stared at the Paver, and as he stared there came a wee while of silence. There was a hush among the loons on the lake, and the wind among the leaves stopped lisping.

"Men," said the Mower, at last. "Now that the Paver has come to himself, I'll tell you how I found this lake. When I started out to meet the dog, the Paver expected, as you all know well, that he was seeing the end of me. Oh, I know what was in his mind when we skidded down the rainbow leg. But that has nothing to do with this story. I met the dog face to face, and I could see from his eye that we were going to do some running."

"Oh," cried Willie the Wisp, "the loons' eggs are bubbling!"

"Good," said the Mower, "just as I said they would."

The Wee Men clapped their hands, and the Meadow Sniffer remarked that the fog from the pot made him dizzy.

"Sit back then," said the Mower. "You're too close to it anyway. But to go on with my story—no more talk from any of you until I finish—as I was about to say, the intention of the dog was to swallow me whole, but I had intentions, too. Said I to myself, 'If he swallows me whole, who will mow the mist off the braes and the bogs?' I was doing some fast thinking, I tell you.

"Then all of a sudden the dog took a lick out of my rainbow cloak. Now I ask you—if he'd licked the cloak clean off of me, where would *I* be?"

"He would have found *yourself* then," said the Weaver.

THE NIGHT OF THE BIG WIND

"Of course he would," put in the Stooker-of-Wheat-Sheaves.

"Oh, go on, go on," urged the Quarryman. "I can't stand much of this."

"Hold on," said the Paver, "that dog must have been color blind, or the loons' eggs wouldn't be boiling."

The Mower glowered at the Paver again. "Do you want to tell this story?" he asked. "Well then, rest your tongue and use your brains a little more. That dog wasn't color blind. The moment he got the taste of my cloak he sprang at me, and I jumped so quickly that I leaped clear out of my mushroom clogs. That gave the dog a chance to smell the clogs: as he did so, he sneezed. By the time he had finished his sneeze, I'd felt for the string around my neck and reached for my magpie's neck-bone. I was just about to throw him the bone when I thought of Limpy.

"All of you remember wee Limpy the Hummer. He was as fine a Wee Man as ever limped over the top of a brae. The only thing the Paver had against him was his humming, and for that he changed him into a humming bird. Well, long, long ago when Limpy was himself, he gave me the magpie's neck-bone. Said he, 'There's no telling how long I'll be Limpy, but I'll give you the neck-bone, anyway. Wear it around your neck and no harm will ever come to you.'

"I looked at the dog and the windowpane stare in his eyes. 'You'll not get this bone!' I shouted. And with that I took to my heels, and he after me. I could feel that dog's hot breath on my bare soles. When I came to the creek, I was so out of breath that I could neither wade it nor jump it. But I had to get across, and the only thing to do was to bridge it. I pulled off my rainbow cloak and flung it across the creek. Then over the bridge I ran to the other side."

The Paver interrupted. "Did the dog go over the rainbow bridge?"

"No," answered the Mower. "He'd have bogged in it if he had."

The Stooker coughed and squinted at the Paver. "You ought to know that," he said.

Willie the Wisp threw a wee handful of fagots under the pot as he said, "The bubbles are bubbling right over the top of the pot."

"Let them bubble," said the Mower. "They'll quiet down soon enough."

THE NIGHT OF THE BIG WIND

Grunty the Fisherman yawned. "I want to know," he said to the Mower, "how you found the loons' eggs and the lake. Did the dog chase you here?"

"He did not," answered the Mower. "When I crossed the bridge I didn't have time to pull my cloak after me, for the dog plunged into the creek and I could see he was bent on a hunt. Instead of being scared I could feel my beard bristle. 'Come on!' I called to the dog. 'If it's a hunt you're after the Midsummer Mower will give it to you.' Then away through the forest I ran again with the dog after me.

"All of a sudden I saw a red fox about four sparrow jumps ahead of me. 'Get out of my way!' I cried to the fox. 'Can't you see there's a big black dog behind me?'

"The fox looked over his shoulder. 'So there is,' he said.

"By this time I'd caught up with him.

" 'He's chasing you,' said the fox.

" 'Of course he is,' I answered sharply.

" 'What's that hanging around your neck?' asked the fox.

" 'It's the neck-bone of a magpie,' said I.

" 'Throw it to me,' said he, 'and you'll run lighter without it.'

" 'And what would you do with it?' I asked.

" 'Oh,' said he, 'just nibble on it for a bit to get an appetite for supper. I'm due at the lake when daylight goes out. But you'll never reach the lake. The dog behind you has his mouth open, and now I see him licking his chops just as if he'd swallowed you whole.'

"I could hear my wee heart rattling in my side, but I quickened my run till I sped like a wisp. The fox kept loping along beside me.

" 'I say,' said he, 'you can't keep up this pace very long. You're lagging like a sloth. Look behind you! The dog is getting ready to spring. Better give me that magpie's neck-bone. It'll be no good to you now, and it'll be a nice nibble for me. I could do you a good turn if you'd give me that bone. I could turn that dog away from you.'

" 'Could you now?' said I. 'Well, if you can do that, why shouldn't I do it myself?'

"With that I cast a skipping glance over my shoulder, and would you believe it? The dog was away far behind me. I looked at the fox. He was watching me out of the corner of his eye. 'Well,' said I, 'something must have soured that dog's taste. I wouldn't be surprised if it was the company I'm with.'

"The cunning melted out of the fox's face. He didn't know what to say.

" 'I'll keep my magpie's neck-bone, thank you,' said I, 'and now that I'm in your company I might as well trot with you to the lake.'

" 'Suit yourself,' he snarled. 'I'll have more than a magpie's neck-bone when we get to the lake.'

" 'Now what do you mean by that?' I asked boldly enough, but with a tremble inside me.

" 'There's loons on the lake,' he answered, 'but none for you—understand that. You'll have to content yourself with what loons' eggs you can find.'

" 'Loons' eggs?' I asked. 'Are they good to eat?'

" 'None better.' He was laughing now. 'But let's get along. I'm tired of talking.'

" 'Just one question,' I said. 'How far are we from the sea?'

" 'A snail's mile, more or less, over the hill to your right.'

"At last we arrived at the lake, just before daylight went out.

" 'Now then,' said the fox, 'I'm off after a loon. You'd better hunt loons' eggs. So along with you, and your magpie's neck-bone.'

"The first thing I found was this pot, on the bank, half full of water. As for the cabin over there, I haven't been into it yet. When the moon came up the lake grew full of moonflakes. So I sang me a song and all the loons on the lake sang, too.

"All at once I heard the fox laugh. 'What are you laughing at?' I called.

" 'Oh,' came back the answer, 'I was just thinking of you and your magpie's neck-bone. Come, gather your loons' eggs over there in the thicket.' "

Willie the Wisp held up his hand and cried, "The fog has gone from the top of the pot, and the bubbles have vanished entirely."

"Good," said the Mower. "Now we'll fill our wee bellies with loons' eggs."

CHAPTER EIGHT

THE CRADLE ROCKER

WHEN they had cooled off, each Wee Man had his loon egg. The Paver, as chief of the clan, demanded two.

"I have to think for all of you," he said, "so I ought to have two loon eggs."

The Weaver looked at the Mower. "How about it?" he asked.

"Give him two," said the Mower. "I figured as

much when I gathered the eggs. But as to the Paver's thinking—well, eat your eggs and take your eyes off the moon, for although we're here, we're nowhere. Yet over the hill is the sea, and beyond that, somewhere, lie our meadows and mists, stray goats and young robins. But how to cross the sea? That bit of thinking will have to come after we've eaten our loon eggs."

The wee Cradle Rocker was the first to finish his egg. "I feel so funny," he said, "I could rock the world's babies to sleep."

Grunty the Fisherman jumped to his feet. "There is something in me that wants to fish," said he. "My wee legs feel as if I had my hip boots on, and what bothers me most—I see fish scales in the moon."

"I, too, feel a bit queer," said the Quarryman. "Could it be the loon egg that I just ate? The desire in me now is to go into a quarry and blast enough rock to build a wee steeple."

"There is more than a loon egg in me," said the Weaver. "I'm full of twitchings. I must do some weaving, or at least a wee bit of darning." He rose to his feet and bowed to the Paver, who was now eating into his second egg. "You don't mind," asked the

84

Weaver, "if I borrow a skein from the moon and weave it into the shadows?"

"Not at all," munched the Paver. "Even I feel as if something were happening."

The Mower plucked a blade of grass and wiped his wee mouth. "How about a song? I'm full of notes, and out they must come."

"Oh, me," whispered the Stooker-of-Wheat-Sheaves. "My cough has sunk with the loon egg I ate, and I miss it. I'm not myself without it."

The Counter-of-Lark-Eggs rose to his feet. "Whist! Don't you hear the larks trilling, and the gurgling song the wee brooks sing?"

"Sit down," ordered the Mower. "Something's astray in all of us."

"I must get to work," cried the Meadow Sniffer, "for the bees are on the primroses, there are spiders on the daisies, and I sniff the briar-patch where the four-leaf clover grows."

The Crane Chaser screamed and jumped to his feet. "Look! Look at all those cranes! I must chase them away, or there won't be a minnow or limpet for stew."

"There, there," said the Mower, "be as calm as you

can. Whatever is in us let's hope it'll pass. The urging in me, strive as I may, is to sing a song of a midsummer night."

As the Paver finished his second egg he rolled over on his back and looked up at the moon. In a wee while he jumped to his feet. "Are the clan all here?" he asked.

"They are," answered the Mower.

"Well, what I want to know is," continued the Paver, "how many of you heard Blaney's rooster crow just now?"

"I'm full to the chin, of hunter's horn echoes," said the Mower, "but I'm not that far gone yet, that I hear Blaney's rooster crow."

The wee Cradle Rocker crept up to the Paver and said with a croon, "I must rock you to sleep, for your eyes are wild and starry."

"Get back!" snapped the Paver. "I'm the chief of the clan, the Paver-of-Caves, that blends white heather with moonflakes. Let one of you deny it, and I'll change you from what you are into something I haven't thought of yet." The Paver parted his long beard in the middle and hooked it over his ears. Then three times he stamped on the ground with his mushroom clogs. "Did you all hear that?" he asked.

"Yes," came the wee groggy voices.

"Well, then," said the Paver, "I know my hearing through the ears of my thinking, and that was Blaney's rooster that crowed."

Behind the Paver, on the lake shore's rim, rose a mocking laugh. The Paver turned around and faced the lake. "Who are you," he shouted, "that dares laugh at the Paver-of-Caves?"

The Mower answered, "That was the fox who laughed, and well he may, with loons on the lake and loons on the land. Look at the Weaver over there, shuttling knots into tree shadows."

"Oh," cried the Stooker-of-Wheat-Sheaves, "look at the moon! She's full of ripe harvest fields."

"Right you are," granted the Mower. "But there is something else up there that my eyes see. I see mist on her braes and mist in her lanes, and here I am without a sickle, and a loon's egg sunk inside me. But I must sing a song or get rid of my egg."

"There'll be no singing," said the Paver, "for there is work to be done."

THE WEE MEN OF BALLYWOODEN

The Cradle Rocker crept over to the pot and addressed the clan. "I must leave you," he wailed, "for far, far away comes the wee wailing of babies."

"There, there," soothed the Mower, "you're a good little man, but you're lost enough as it is, without losing yourself entirely. Long, long ago, Limpy the Hummer gave me a bit of advice. Said he, 'If your mind ever wobbles, chew the heart of a leaf from a crab-apple tree.' It's good advice, too, but where might there be a crab-apple tree?"

"Silence, all of you!" commanded the Paver. "I must talk to myself, for there're two of me here, and I'm not sure which one I am."

The Mower whispered to the Quarryman, "The Paver is in a bad way with *two* loon eggs inside him."

"What do you say to coaxing him out of the moonlight?" asked the Quarryman. "Look at his wee belly bulging."

The Paver began to argue with himself as to whether or not he was just one of the clan, or the Paver-of-Caves who blended white heather with moonflakes. Then all of a sudden he gave a command. "I'll test myself," said he, "and see just who I am.

Every man of you take off your rainbow cloaks and put them into the pot."

Every man obeyed. The pot was heaped full with rainbow cloaks.

"Now," said the Paver to Willie the Wisp, "hold your wee torch under the pot."

But the loon's egg that Willie had eaten, instead of going to his head, went into his light.

The Mower nudged Grunty the Fisherman. "Are your eyes all right? I see a blaze coming out of Willie's wee hand."

The Fisherman only grunted. "I put my cloak into the pot," said he, "and isn't that enough? My business is not to answer questions, for I'm far too busy counting my fish."

"Hm," said the Mower, "there must have been two yolks in your loon egg."

The Paver folded his arms across his wee breast. "Now then," said he, "we'll soon see who's the Paver-of-Caves."

The Wee Men encircled the pot and every eye was upon it. Pretty soon, without any warning, the head of a rainbow rose out of the pot. It wriggled, uncertain of what course to take.

"Stand back, men!" shouted the Paver. "Don't get in its way, for if my thinking is right, it should arch toward the sea."

"It can't," said the Mower, "for there's a brae in the way."

"But it will," snapped the Paver. "Isn't it my rainbow?"

"You have a cloak in it," said the Mower, "and what's left belongs to the clan."

"Hold on," cried the Weaver, "the colors are all wrong in it! The pink has smudged the yellow, and the green is dyeing the blue. From the looks of it, it's not to be trusted."

"Nobody but a loon," put in the Mower, "would think of boiling rainbow cloaks."

"The Paver's mind is clouded," said the Quarryman, "and if I'm seeing right, the head of his rainbow looks straggly."

As they talked, the bulk of the rainbow trailed out of the pot. Up it rose, straight over their heads.

The Mower looked at the Paver. "If you are the Paver-of-Caves," said he, "put a curve into that rainbow."

"He can't," spoke up the Stooker-of-Wheat-

Sheaves, "for we wore the curves out of it, and now with the boiling, the rainbow has only one leg to stand on."

The Paver's pale face showed a thousand summers of wrinkles. He opened his mouth to give a command, then closed it again. A shout went up from the wee men, for the foot of the rainbow was lifting itself out of the pot. Slowly it soared upward, and tears began to drop from the Paver's eyes.

"I don't know where I left myself," he cried. "I can't be the Paver-of-Caves after all." And he wept so hard that most of the Wee Men joined him.

"The rainbow's gone, and so are our rainbow cloaks!"

"No more of that tear splashing!" shouted the Mower. "The first thing we know the lake will run over its banks. We're all lost, but we're no worse off than before we lost our cloaks."

Grunty the Fisherman whose eyes were as dry as the wing of a fly, spoke up that all might hear. Said he, "Since eating that loon's egg, my sight is so much the better, and I can see the moon is fishing to-night and has hooked the head of the rainbow."

"Let her have it," said the Mower. "It's only a moon-bow, anyway."

The Paver dried his eyes. "There is one more test I want to make," said he, "and if I can't locate myself after that, then I'll be satisfied. Every man of you march down to the lake and load your wee backs with moonflakes. Carry them to the cabin over there and I'll try a bit of paving."

"But where's your tamper?" the Mower asked.

"Never mind my tamper," answered the Paver. "I'll pave with my mushroom clogs."

Load after load of moonflakes the wee men carried to the cabin. The Paver tamped and tamped with his mushroom clogs but not a flake could he manage to stick to the floor. He was choked in moonflakes, so he called a halt.

"Wherever the other half of me went," said he, "there went the Paver-of-Caves. I'm not he, and whoever I am, the fleece of the moonflakes is smothering me."

The Mower dropped his load and spoke. Said he, "These moonflakes are inflated, and it's limpets horns you need to spike them."

"Don't tell me what I need," snapped the Paver.

THE NIGHT OF THE BIG WIND

The wee Cradle Rocker yawned. "I've got to do one of two things," he said, "either cry or sleep, and I can do one just as quickly as the other."

The Quarryman stretched himself. "I'm not against a bit of crying myself," said he. "Nothing seems to matter. We're lost and we're lonesome. Now that we've eaten those loon eggs I have a pain in my belly."

"Whist!" whispered the Paver. "Don't mention pains or we'll all be feeling them. Crowd into the cabin, all of you, and we'll bolster ourselves with moonflakes and take a sound sleep."

Then every one of the Wee Men heaped for himself a mound of moonflakes. As the Mower settled himself, he untied the magpie's neck-bone from around his neck and stuck it in his mouth. The Paver was watching him.

"Why do you do that?" he asked.

The Mower took the magpie's neck-bone out of his mouth and let a wee laugh out of him as he answered the Paver. "Did you think that the red fox showed me this lake and loons' eggs for nothing?" Then he stuck the magpie's neck-bone into his mouth again and lay back on his heap of moonflakes.

THE WEE MEN OF BALLYWOODEN

"Off to sleep, all of you!" commanded the Paver.

In a little while a gentle sound, like the susking of a wee river, came from the depths of the moonflakes and once again the Wee Men were lost in the land of sleep.

CHAPTER NINE

OLD Danny O'Fay was up on a ladder, thatching the roof of his hut, while Jerry his donkey was eating the grass along the side of the road. Old Danny, for lack of company, was talking to himself.

"Ah, what a fine morning it is. Sure the griddle in the sun would bake a bannock of bread, and as for the sea, it's oversleeping itself. And I have a mind, before it wakes up, to take myself down and cut a few panes for my window out of it. Sure it would never miss a few panes of glass. When I think of that night, and the way it carried on, with its coughing and roaring, and the extravagant way it was spilling itself! Ah well, the poor devil in it must be sleeping to-day."

The donkey flattened his ears along the back of his neck and, straightening his tail, heehawed.

"Now, Jerry," said Danny, "what ails you? With green grass up to your ankles, and not an ounce of work have you been doing these many days. Well, if your song gives you pleasure, heehaw all you like. But if it's a welcome heehaw you're giving for something my eyes don't see, then more power to ye, for it's lonesome I am since the Wee Men are gone. But I'm not complaining. There's a fist full of flour and an old drake left. And although my pipe is empty, the smudge in the bowl of it smells of tobacco. And as to the taste of fish—sure 'n' my mouth is through watering for them. Try as I may with my thoughts and my thatching, I can't keep my mind off the Wee Men. Poor darlings, where are they at all? May the serpent in the wind choke itself on a mouthful of the world, and if that can't be, well, it's not cursing I am the day. But may the head of the wind serpent chase its tail around and around in a circle, and around again, as long as Time has time for that and nothing else.

"But here I am fretting, with work to be done, and it's thinking of myself I am. Tut, tut, Danny O'Fay, don't allow old age to seep into your marrow. What if your joints do squeak like dry axles? Isn't the heart in ye murmuring ripples of youth? There's not a complaint out of one of the Wee Men, I'm sure, whereever they are.

"But my thoughts won't behave, try as I may, for I'm afraid the Big Wind strayed away with them. Sure they may be up in the sky, skinning their wee knuckles from rapping on Heaven's door. May my whisper reach the ears of the doorkeeper up there, and if he's a man at all, he'll turn the key and let them in, for I know and they know the struggles they have with us mortals down here.

"But here I am, letting my thoughts gallop away with me. It's thatching I should be doing, instead of staring away into nothing. Sure there's no comfort in that, any more than there is in the last bit of bannock."

Danny's old drake squawked up at him from the foot of the ladder.

"Get out of my sight!" shouted Danny. "If you knew the bad thoughts I had of you, it's far you'd be traveling, and be losing yourself entirely. Away to the bog with you and quack to the frogs. There is emptiness inside of me. I may forget myself and pluck you, and drop you into the pot."

While Danny and the drake were arguing Mrs. Blaney came along the road with a shawl over her shoulders and the worry of the county in her face. She stopped and spoke.

"Is that you up there I'm seeing, Danny O'Fay?"

"Sure and it's not the wraith of me you're seeing, Mrs. Blaney."

"Come down out of that, Danny, for it's a word I want with you."

Then as Danny came down from the ladder, "Ah, it's terrible times we're having," said she, "since the night of the Big Wind. My rooster, the pride of the parish, hasn't crowed since."

"So I've been hearing," said Danny.

"Ah, but that's not the worst," she went on. "The goats don't come home to be milked any more, and the fogs in the mornings are as thick as frog spawns. The schoolmaster complains of the children being late. That's terrible in itself, Danny O'Fay, but when you think of the hay that's scattered over the county, with the farmers fighting over its ownership! And that's not the worst. There isn't a young mother hereabouts that hasn't a child without its earache, since that night. And the mothers, God bless them, have to rock them all night! Isn't it strange, Danny, the way things have changed here?"

"It is, it is, Mrs. Blaney," said he, "but it's not to be wondered at."

She laid her hand on his shoulder as he sat on the rung of the ladder. "Danny, it's whispered around that all the fish in the sea blew away. Now, Danny O'Fay, I have my eye on your eye. Is it true there's no fish in the sea?"

"Mrs. Blaney, it's not for me to say what is and what isn't. But from the way the sea behaved the night of the Big Wind, I'd not be surprised at anything."

"But, Danny, the sea's not to blame."

"Of course it is, Mrs. Blaney. Sure 'n' it didn't have to notice the Big Wind at all. But it did go ranting and raving, and I suppose the fish grew tired of it and swum away to another sea that had the grace and goodness to mind its own business and welcome the fish that swim in its waters."

"Oh, Danny O'Fay, don't tell me that! What's to become of us, with no fish in the sea? The wind tore the kale out by the roots, and the green tops of the potatoes are wilted and dying. And the pigs squeal around with their sides hanging empty. Ah, strange things do be happening! Could it be that there's a curse on us, Danny O'Fay?"

"Well," said Danny slowly, "things may be different, if ever *they* come back again."

"Now what do you be talking about, Danny O'Fay?"

"Oh, it's just a word with myself I be having, Mrs. Blaney."

"Now, Danny, there's something about you that we whisper awhile, and that's why I'm here this morning. Word has been passed around that your donkey no longer trots the roads at night, and pious men have been keeping an eye on your hut. They say that ne'er a wee light do they see any more. Danny, the prayers of the parish were never so powerful, but,

God forgive me, there's an ear somewhere that's hard of hearing. Did I tell ye that the cows don't give down their milk entirely? We churn and churn and not a skimming of butter comes from the milk.

"Now, Danny O'Fay, I've told you the worst, and it's helpless we are. So I've come to you, for a word of advice. But first let me promise you, if ever the fish gets back in your cart, we'll welcome your song and buy all your fish. And there'll never be a question as to whether you buy from fishermen or if you never fish yourself. Now, Danny, what's to be done with the curse on the county?"

Danny arose from the rung of the ladder. "Mrs. Blaney," he said, "it's poor advice that I have to give, for I'm heartsore and lonely, these days. But go home, Mrs. Blaney, and tether your cows in deep clover. And as for your goats that's gone astray, maybe they'll be driven home some day. When ye get over yonder by the bend in the road, throw three clods into the sea. And hereafter, never bar your door at night, and always leave a wee bit of food on the door-step. Good-morning to you, Mrs. Blaney."

"Good-morning to you, Danny O'Fay."

Danny stuck a bundle of straw under his arm and

started up the ladder again. As he was laying a bunch of thatch, ready for the mud, a wee humming bird buzzed around his head.

"Well, well," said Danny, "in the name of the highest mountain in the world, where did you come from? Is it looking for straw to build a wee nest you are? Now, stop your humming, so I can hear myself think. Where did you come from at all? Bad cess to you, keep away from my ears. Can't you see that I'm busy thatching my roof?

"But there's one thing I'd like to ask you, humming bird though you are. How did you escape the Big Wind? Ah, sure, what ails the mind of me, talking to the likes of you? If it's a bit of straw ye want, here, take it and be off with ye. Look at the sun how high he's rearing. Soon he'll be canting to the westward. And here I've been sitting and sitting all the morning, listening to Mrs. Blaney and the whines of the parish. Now get away from me I tell you, before I forget you're an innocent humming bird."

But the humming bird was not to be driven off. He buzzed and hummed around old Danny's head.

"Look here," said Danny at last, "my patience is strained to the breaking point now. One of us must get off the roof. The first thing you know I'll be hailing a hawk from the sky. It isn't so much that I mind your buzzing and humming. It's your flying that bothers me so. You fly backwards as well as forwards and no matter if I look up or down or sideways, you're always there. I tell you it upsets me, with your thousand fast running cogs in your wings. I've known birds in my times, and birds that ate out of my hand, mind you, but your like I've never known before. You seem to have no fear at all."

The humming bird lit on the rung of the ladder. As Danny looked at it he sighed. "Ah, and what a darling you are, after all. Sure I ought to get down off this ladder and dig you a worm. It's the Wee Men, God bless them, that you ought to know. They're not exactly the kind of men that a man can talk much to; their wee hands are small, but they'd always reach out to a creature like you.

"Now that I see the wee eyes of you, it's strange the way they look at me. You are a humming bird. I'll wager a turf fire on that. But where did you come from, this time of year? Answer me that. Ah, there you sit, and not a peep out of you. And I go on talking, with work to be done. But if I wasn't talking to you, I'd be talking to the morning, anyway, for talk I must. The heart of me is heavy, ever since the night of the Big Wind. I miss my drop of goat's milk in the mornings. And the fire isn't lit any more. And if there's a fish in the sea, I don't know it at all."

The humming bird sat staring into old Danny's eyes, and Danny stared back as he went on talking. "You're a queer little bird. There's something about you that charms me. Come down off that rung and let me scratch your wee head. Sure and I wouldn't hurt you, any more than I would one of *them*. Oh, don't look so saucy. It's the Wee Men I'm talking about. Well, stay where you are, if it pleases you better. And since you're a good listener, I'll tell you some more.

"I have searched every pocket of my mind, trying to find out where the Wee Men are, and I've come to believe that the Big Wind blew them away from this land. Ah, what a terrible calamity it is, not to me alone, but to the whole county as well. Everything has gone wrong in it since *they* strayed away. My thoughts are like stirabout. The more I stir them the thicker they get. There's not a single night that I don't put out my empty pipe, and sure 'n' empty it is in the morning. Now if they were about, my pipe would be full of tobacco. Ah, what's going to become of me at all? I have tried a few prayers since they blew away, for the safe return of them all. But a wee man is deaf to prayers that come from me, or the likes of me. They have their own ways, and helpful ways they are to some of us about here. If only they'd come back again there would be a few summers left in me yet.

"I have talked and talked to that old drake of mine, trying to get something into his head. 'Fly away,' says I, 'and find *them*, for they know the lone note in your quack. I took the old drake up in my arms and pointed across the sea. 'Do you see that bit of land over there?' says I. 'It lies waist deep, there in the sea. They must be over there or somewhere.' And up in the air I flung him. 'Now be gone with you!' says I. Ah, but did he go? He did not. He flew to the bog and the frogs, the blackguard."

"There now," went on Danny, "that's enough talk for one morning. But I haven't begrudged you my time, for it's dying I was to have a talk with even the likes of you."

Danny moved down the ladder a rung to reach for

his bundle of straw. He pulled it toward him to begin thatching again.

"There's something else I want to say to you," he
said to the humming bird.

He looked up to the top rung of the ladder. But
no humming· bird was there. Danny scratched his
head.

"I wonder," said he, "if I'm myself at all. Wasn't
I talking to a bird that had eyes that spoke words?
Well, if I wasn't, then I'm not thatching the roof of
my hut. But to work with you, Danny O'Fay. If ye
have no more distractions, ye'll finish your thatching
to-day."

CHAPTER TEN

IN THE cabin by the lake the Wee Men were
sleeping and sleeping, and it seemed as if they
never would wake up. One evening, after the day had
shut its door, night, with long lilting shadows, strolled
into the forest. There was a light in the cabin, and it
came from the moonflakes that the Wee Men were
sleeping on. It was not much of a light, but it was
enough to guide a humming bird through the door.

Around and around it flew, buzzing and buzzing in the ears of the Wee Men, but not a stir came from one of them. They were deep in the slumber of their loon egg tilt.

At last the humming bird lit on the wee stubby nose of the Midsummer Mower. He began to scratch and scratch, until the Mower stirred. Then in another little while he opened his eyes and stared at the humming bird scratching his nose. After another wee while he opened his mouth, reached in with his hand, and pulled out the magpie's neck-bone. When he had tied it securely around his own wee neck, he rose to his feet. Then he kicked a few stray moonflakes out of his way. His tongue was a bit thick but he managed to speak.

Said he to the humming bird, "Are you a wee loon that's trying to lay a wee egg on the top of my nose? If you are, it'll do you no good, for there's no room for another loon egg inside or out of me. Get off my nose, or I'll call the red fox."

The humming bird opened its bill and began to speak like a Wee Man. "Are you so far off," he said, "that you don't know Limpy the Hummer?"

The Mower looked dazed. "Limpy the Hummer?"

said he. "Limpy, that was changed by the Paver into a humming bird?"

"I'm the very same Limpy."

The Mower reached up to his nose and took hold of the bird. Then he stared into its eyes. Limpy winked through the eyes of the bird.

"Don't you remember me now?" said he.

"Sure and I do," answered the Mower. "How could I forget that wink? Do you remember the night there was no moon and I fell off the donkey? Limpy, oh, Limpy, if you had a wee hand I'd shake it! I want to sing!"

"Wake them up!" ordered the Hummer. "I'm winging lost news to the clan. Is that the Paver over there, with his feet propped up and his head on the Weaver's chest?"

"That's himself. I'll work on him first."

While the humming bird perched on a rafter, the Mower shook the Paver. He pulled his long beard, he tickled his nose, he shouted, "Lost news!" in his ear. Not as much as a grunt came from the Paver.

The Mower looked up at the humming bird. "What do you think of that?" he asked.

"I have an idea," said the Hummer. "Wake up the

Cradle Rocker and have him cry the whole clan awake."

"Why didn't I think of that!" said the Mower. "The Cradle Rocker must be bubbling in tears. But how shall I waken him?"

"Cry, whine, croon in his ear like a baby. He'll come to himself with that," said the Hummer.

The Mower went from one Wee Man to another around the cabin, and at last he came upon the Cradle Rocker. He was sleeping in a cradle of moonflakes. The Mower stooped over till his mouth touched the Cradle Rocker's wee hairy ear. Then he crooned and he babbled and he cooed like a baby. All of a sudden the wee Cradle Rocker opened his eyes and looked around him. The Mower patted him on the head.

"Cry!" urged the Mower. "Cry like you never cried before! Limpy the Hummer is here. He carries lost news for the clan."

"But I can't cry," whined the Cradle Rocker, "for sleep makes me tearless."

"Come, come," said the Mower. "You're not sleeping now. Where do you think you are?"

"I know," nodded the Cradle Rocker. "I'm resting now after a night's hard rocking of something."

"Don't you know you're lost, and the clan is sleeping and can't wake up?"

"Yes, yes," said the Cradle Rocker. "I remember. I ate a loon's egg. Now I do want to cry."

"That's a good little man," said the Mower. "I knew you would cry when you came to yourself."

The Cradle Rocker began to cry, softly at first, as if some of the clan had stepped on his toes. Then louder the crying came out of him, till the tears from his eyes started to melt the moonflakes.

"Louder!" shouted the Mower. "Don't you know you're the lost Rocker?"

The Cradle Rocker opened his mouth wide and the like of such crying was never heard before. The Mower glanced up at the Hummer.

"Do you think," said he, "there is any danger of him crying the moon out of the sky?"

"It might move her a bit," admitted the Hummer.

By this time the wee Cradle Rocker's tears were running wee rivers on the cabin floor, and a stream of them flowed under the rump of the Paver. Not till then did he awake, and he sat up with a start.

"Where are we now?" he asked. "Can anyone answer me that?"

THE WEE MEN OF BALLYWOODEN

"Get to your feet," said the Mower, "and shake the hot tears from yourself."

"Before I do anything," said the Paver, "tell me, what ails the Cradle Rocker? He must stop that crying, for I have to think where all of us are."

Nobody answered him, and the Cradle Rocker kept on crying till there wasn't an empty snail shell of tears left in him. By that time every man in the clan was awake.

"Gather around, men," ordered the Mower. "There's news for the clan. Limpy the Hummer is here. Up there he sits, on the rafter."

When the Wee Men's eyes lit on the Hummer, they clapped their wee hands and cheered. The Paver was so overcome that he turned a complete somersault in a pool of tears. When he recovered his dignity he silenced the clan.

"Are you forgetting, men, where you are?" he said. "No more of this cheering or clapping of hands till we hear from Limpy the Hummer."

A cloak of silence settled down on them, and the only light now came from the glistening eyes of the clan.

THE NIGHT OF THE BIG WIND

The Paver threw back his head and spoke to the Hummer.

"Limpy," he said, "how did you find the lost clan?"

The humming bird opened his lance-like bill and spoke from his perch on the rafter.

"I found you," he said, "through Danny's old drake. Over the sea I flew, till I met a straight rainbow, and, said I to myself, 'They must be here, or somewhere about.'"

"Hm, hm," said the Paver as he glanced at the Mower. "Go on."

"Below me I saw the lake, with the loons swimming in it. I circled about till I saw a red fox coming out of this cabin. 'What could he be doing in there?' I thought."

The Mower felt of the magpie's neck-bone around his neck and nudged the Weaver.

"It was then I flew into this cabin and found you," said Limpy.

A wail came from the Quarryman. "But how are we going to get back to our land?"

"That's easy enough," answered Limpy. "The Paver has power, and I know the way."

A chorus of cries went up from the clan. "The Paver has no power! We're no better off than before you found us!" And their tears began to flow. The only dry eyes in the cabin were those of the Hummer and the Cradle Rocker.

All of a sudden the humming bird flew off the rafter and around the Midsummer Mower, humming and humming.

"What's that around your neck?" he asked.

"Why, that," said the Mower, "is the magpie's neck-bone that you gave me a long time ago."

"Hm," said the Hummer and he winked at the Paver.

The Paver-of-Caves gave one jump and landed beside the Mower. The Paver's eyes glowed with the color of a dawn. The Mower wilted under that stare. Then without any questioning, the Paver undid the magpie's neck-bone from around the Mower's neck. And he rubbed it and rubbed it between his wee hands, the while he muttered strange words. And the Hummer kept humming, "Hmm, hmm, hmm, hmm."

In no more time than it takes a bullfrog to croak, something happened. The Paver's beard began to wiggle, and the Wee Men dried their eyes. What they saw was something turning in the hands of the Paver, and it was nothing less than a wee tamper of moonflakes, with a bend in the middle.

"Oh, oh," cried the Mower, "where's my magpie's neck-bone?"

"Hm, hm," hummed the Hummer.

Then the Paver-of-Caves, blender of white heather and moonflakes, spoke in his cave-like voice.

"Every man of you," he commanded, "get out of this cabin and line up on the bank of the lake. I must be alone, to do a bit of flighty thinking."

The clan trailed out of the cabin, and the Hummer hummed on the wing. When they had lined themselves up on the lake shore, the Stooker-of-Wheat Sheaves coughed.

"Anyway," said he, "I'm glad my cough is back."

"I'm hoping," said the Mower, "this is not the last rift from the loons' eggs that he ate."

"Hmm, hmm," hummed Limpy the Hummer.

In a little while the Paver came running out of the cabin. The first thing he did was to order the Mower to stand back by himself and away from the clan. Then he called to the Hummer.

"Wing yourself up," he commanded, "as high as the tallest tree, and let me know if the moon is coming."

Limpy hummed up and pretty soon he hummed down, and he lit on the Paver's head.

"Yes, the moon is up," said he, "but her right ear is gone."

"That's nothing for her," said the Paver, "she'll grow it soon again. But, Limpy, stay up there on top of my head. Now then, men," he said to the clan, "all you have to do, when I make the change, is to follow the leader. Keep your eyes on me, all of you."

To the Midsummer Mower he said, "Stand back a little farther and close your eyes."

Then the Paver took a firm hold of the wee bended tamper and began to spin. And he spun so fast that the wind from him rustled the leaves of the trees. All of a sudden he stopped and shouted:

"GRAY GEESE!"

At that every man of the clan turned into a gray goose. The Paver ran to where the Mower stood. He was now a big gray gander, flapping his wings. The Paver jumped astride of the gander's neck and spoke to Limpy, on top of his head.

THE NIGHT OF THE BIG WIND

"All ready?"

"All ready," hummed Limpy the Hummer.

The Paver held the tamper between the eyes of the gander. "Away with you now," said he. "I'll do the steering, and you follow the point of the tamper."

Away flew the gander over the tops of the trees, honking to the flock behind him.

"Are they coming?" asked the Paver of the Hummer.

"They are," hummed Limpy, "every one of them."

"Are we winging for Ballywooden?" then asked the Paver.

"Not quite," answered Limpy. "Sheer away a mite from the eaves of the moon."

The Paver ported his tamper on the top of the gander's head, and the gander honked, "Aye, aye!"

Later that night a flock of geese lit beside old Danny's hut. The Paver dismounted and changed them all into what they were before.

"Away with you now," said the Paver to the clan, "and do the work that's waiting for you."

"How about me?" said the wee humming bird from the top of his head.

THE WEE MEN OF BALLYWOODEN

"Will you promise to smother your humming?" the Paver asked.

"I promise," said the Hummer.

"Well, then," said the Paver, and he changed him into a Wee Man again.

Then away went Limpy the Hummer, with the wee limp in his leg, smothering his hum over the moonlit braes.

CHAPTER ELEVEN

A S THE new day pulled its window blinds up, Blaney's rooster crowed three times and every man within hearing jumped out of his bed.

Danny O'Fay rubbed his eyes and threw his quilt back off his old thin shins. "Is it dreaming I be," he said to himself, "or is it hearing Blaney's rooster crow I am? Crow or no crow," said he, "it's up I'm getting anyway."

As he pulled on his brown breeches, he heard Jerry his donkey crunching in his stall.

He scratched his wisp of hair. "Jerry," said he, "I must be all twisted this morning. I'm hearing things and seeing nothing. Sure and I know there is not a thimbleful of oats within a mile of you, and I could have sworn I heard Blaney's rooster crow, into the bargain."

Then, as he stooped down to lace his boots, his old eyes saw a wee fire in the grate.

"By the power of the sea and the height of the mountains, it's a jig I'll be doing this morning!"

And up jumped Danny O'Fay and jigged by the light that came in through the window. Then he heard a wee rap on the door.

"By the light that shines," he cried, "this is the morning of mornings!"

He opened the door. There on the step lay his clay pipe full of tobacco. A smile came into his face of plowed wrinkles.

"A fine day to yez all!" said he. "And while I don't see a man of ye, God bless every one of ye!"

He picked up his pipe and walked out to his cart. There were fish that were fat in it, and every one of them fresh from the sea. Old Danny hurried into his hut and spoke to his donkey.

"Come, Jerry," said he, "get into your harness. There's fish in the cart; there's a fire in the grate, and a pot of red tea on the hob."

Later that morning old Danny drove up to Mrs. Blaney's, shouting his song: "Fresh fish! Fresh fish! Fresh fish from the sea, every one of them!"

Mrs. Blaney came down the garden walk with a smile on her face.

"Good-morning to you, Danny O'Fay."

"Good-morning to you, Mrs. Blaney. Is it fish you'll be wanting to-day?"

"Troth and it is, Danny O'Fay. Did I tell you the news?" she went on.

"You did not," answered old Danny.

"In the first place, the rooster crowed this morning. And that's not all, by any means. The cows, to a cow, gave down all their milk, and would you believe it, all the stray goats are home. And the mists in the meadows have lanes again. I'll be taking a dozen of your fish, Danny O'Fay—the ones with the big scales on them."

"To be sure, Mrs. Blaney. Help yourself to what you want."

"Has there been any change in things for you, Danny?"

"There has, Mrs. Blaney. I can hear the larks singing, and smell the primroses, and feel the sea's breath on my cheek. And there's grand notes in the lilt of the wind. Good-morning to you, Mrs. Blaney. Get up, Jerry! Fresh fish! Fresh fish! Fresh out of the sea, every one of them!"

COGGELTY - CURRY

CHAPTER ONE

IT WAS whispered that on the night before the full of the moon the Wee Men's Jackdaw had flown away. Anyway, the Jackdaw was missing, and so were other things.

There was a farm close by the strand, and when the farmer got up that morning he went out to the stable to harness his horses for plowing. As he opened the stable door he spoke to the big black mare: "Move your rump around," said he, "and let the daylight in."

It was when she moved that he noticed that all the hairs in her tail were gone; plucked as clean as the moss off a rock. "Ho, ho," said the farmer. Then he looked at his other horse. Bare and bald that tail was, too.

"Well, well," said the farmer, scratching his head, "I'd give the bullock's horn to know where the hair in your tails went, for not a sight of one do I see in the stable. Strange things are happening these days, so they are, but I'll bandage your tails so you won't catch cold. For plow you shall, and work I must."

Later that day, when the sun was over the big oak tree, the farmer at his plowing was wondering why his wife didn't blow the bullock's horn to call him home for dinner. Never had the like of this happened to him before. The horses nickered and wagged their bandaged tails, for they were hungry, too. So the farmer unhitched and rode home, talking to himself the while of things that are, and things that are not.

His wife was sitting on the doorstep, rocking herself, in sorrow.

"Why didn't you blow the bullock's horn?" shouted the farmer, angrily.

"The bullock's horn is gone!" wailed his wife. "And that's not all. Two of my new spools of black thread are gone, too. But whist!" she said, "I have a whisper for you. The blind fiddler and his boy just went by. Said the fiddler's boy to me, 'I'll be telling you a secret. The Wee Men's Jackdaw is missing, and I'm hunting the fiddler's bow. Not a word to anyone,' he warned, 'but sleep with a walnut between your toes if you want to keep the pewit's wing in your bonnet.' "

"Where is the fiddler's boy now?" the farmer asked his wife. "I'd like a word with him."

"He's away to the crossroads," she answered, "and him laughing, and the blind fiddler crying about the lost bow to his fiddle. Put your horses away and come in to your dinner. The fish is roasted and the potatoes are laughing and the tea has been boiling for an hour. And when you've filled yourself full you can take yourself off to the market and buy me the wee-est walnut you can find, for it's small toes I do be having. The fiddler's boy had a wink in his eye, and it's me pewit's wing I'll be keeping." Then as the farmer drove his horses off to the stable she called after him, "Say, what have you done with the horses' tails?"

"Ask the fiddler's boy," he answered, and to himself he muttered, "the Jackdaw gone, black thread, hair, and worst of all, the bullock's horn. What would *they* be wanting with that?"

CHAPTER TWO

THAT evening, when the sun went down behind
the mountain, and the farmer's rooster crowed
good-night, a big round moon came up out of the sea.
When the stars came out, the big ones winked at the
little ones. The sea was calm. Not a waft of wind was
there, to make the ripples sing. Along the shore,
where rocks threw shadows, the Wee Sailors' ships
were being made ready for a voyage in search of the

137

missing Jackdaw. Not only had the Jackdaw disappeared, but the wee bagpipes were missing, too, and what could be worse than that, for the Wee Men had to have bagpipes to pipe more than the night away. And who could have taken them but the Jackdaw? They knew well enough that the Jackdaw was always lifting things that didn't belong to him, and besides, he talked too much. Look at the fiddler's boy. He seemed to know all about their doings as soon as they did themselves.

And now dozens of the Wee Men were swarming aboard their ships, none of them any bigger than a lady-thumb banana. They ran here and they ran there, like so many busy ants getting into action. So complete were their plans that, when the farmer's wife went to bed that night, her ear was tickled with a wee besom, and she turned over, letting the walnut slide out from between her toes, while a Wee Man, dressed in a moonlight pullover, plucked the pewit's wing from her best bonnet and ran with it to the water's edge. There a wee boatman sculled him out to one of the big ships. All was ready, but they had to wait for the moon to lift the rock shadows from off their ships.

COGGELTY-CURRY

In a hut overlooking the sea lived the blind fiddler and his boy.

"What's that I smell cooking?" asked the fiddler.

"A pot of cockles from the rocks," answered the boy.

"And who could have gathered them," said the fiddler, "and us tramping the highways all day, hunting the lost bow to my fiddle? If I don't find it, it's ruined we are. There's not a penny in the house, and it's starved we'll be, if I can't play my fiddle."

The fiddler began to cry, and the boy went to his side.

"There, there," he said, "don't worry at all."

The fiddler put out his hand to pat the boy's head. "What!" he exclaimed. "Who cut your hair?"

"Don't know that either," answered the boy. "It was cut when I got up this morning."

"Well, well," whined the fiddler, "what are we coming to? The bow gone, hair cut, and cockles cooking on the fire. Give me my supper before I fall asleep. It's a long walk we'll be having to-morrow, and it's rest I need to-night."

The blind fiddler never ate a better supper in his

life, and he said so. When the boy put him to bed he asked the fiddler, "Do you hear the singing?"

"Tut, tut," said the fiddler, "what nonsense is playing around in your head? It's the whistling curlews you hear."

"No," said the boy, "they're gone, too."

"Go to sleep," said the fiddler, "I've heard enough for a night. It's turnips we'll have to eat to-morrow."

The boy blew out the candle and lay down by the hobs. He covered himself with the fiddler's coat and was soon fast asleep.

CHAPTER THREE

AS THE moon lifted the rock shadows from off the wee ships, ten of them showed themselves; all abreast, ready for the command to set off. There wasn't a ship among them much bigger than a Turk's boot, the prows of them curling up like toes. Their hulls were studded with dolphin scales to give them speed, and each ship carried two masts; wishbones of cuckoos they were, fastened to the keelson. Perched on the prow of every ship was a curlew, ready to take wing and tow the ships out to sea. The towline was a hundred feet of black spool thread. One end was tied around the bird's toes and the other end was fastened with a good stout hitch to a wishbone mast.

The Wee Men were jumping over one another in their excitement to get away. At last, out of one of the cabins came the Pilot. He was being carried by four Wee Men on the pewit's wing. Down they sat him, beside the mast.

"What!" he cried. "No flags up yet?" He jumped to his feet and clicked his heels together. He was wearing red boots that reached to his knees. On his head he wore a white tam-o'-shanter with a potato apple for a tassel. A green cloak hung loose around his shoulders.

"Up with the flags!" he commanded. "We'll never get anywhere without flags." Then he sat down again on the pewit's wing and ordered the compass to be brought to him.

In no time at all flags were running up to the tip-top of the wishbone masts.

"Who made those flags?" roared the Pilot. "There's not enough yellow in them."

"I—I cut them out of an evening rainbow," answered a thick-around-the-middle sailor.

"Well, the next time you make any flags," said the Pilot, "slice them out of a morning rainbow."

A Wee Man came hurrying with the compass and laid it down carefully alongside the Pilot. The compass was nothing more than a sea bubble, cradled in an empty limpet shell. All the Pilot had to do was to keep the bubble balanced so that the wee six-pointed star would be reflected in it. And the star would point the way to wherever the Jackdaw might be.

All was ready now. The Pilot reached for the bullock's horn and blew one long blast. At that signal the curlews took to the wing and flew ahead, slowly at first, until the towlines began to pull on their toes. When the ships began to move, side by side, the Pilot blew two long blasts from the bullock's horn. The curlews were off now through the moonlight, with the wee ships in tow.

"Music! Music!" cried the Pilot. "The wee star is wiggling and hard to keep in the bubble!"

At that appeared a Wee Man with the blind fiddler's bow in his hand. The Musician's red hair and beard were curly, and both parted in the middle. He wore a blue suit that fitted him tightly, like a skin, and the calves of his legs were bulged from marking time. Up to the wishbone mast he walked, with great dignity, and there he took his stand, where the moon's skeins were strained. He pulled the blind fiddler's bow across the moon skeins, and the like of such music had never been heard before. The wee fiddler was at his best with the fiddler's bow, and the moon high, and full of rosined silver.

Louder and louder swelled the strains. The crew of the wee ships stroked their beards, while they stared upward, moonstruck. Fish of all scales stuck their heads out of the sea to listen to the music. Even the codfish, from sixty fathoms deep, came up to hear the music, while the porpoises whirled a misty spray around the ships. And the green turtles, resting their necks on the backs of some lazy seals, lay comfortably listening as they dozed.

The Pilot blew a short blast on the bullock's horn. "That will do!" he called to the Musician. "What do you think you're playing? We'll be running into a whale or something if you cast a spell over us. Play the Sunken Reef Hornpipe. It's speed we need, if we're going to find our own wee bagpipes."

So the fiddler switched into a lively air. And as the music quickened, wee clogs beat time on the ships' decks, and wee hands began to clap and fingers to snap as they swung one another around to the tune of the Sunken Reef Hornpipe. For that was the tune they liked best.

CHAPTER FOUR

~AND THE SQUARE SAILS WERE SET ON THE WISH~BONE MASTS·

A S THE curlews towed the ships past the light-
house, the keeper of the light spoke to his
helper. "Say," he said, "I felt a puff of wind."

"How could that be?" questioned his helper.
"There isn't a cloud in the sky, nor a ripple on the sea.
You couldn't have felt any wind."

"Don't argue with me," said the keeper. "If that
wasn't wind, what was it?"

THE WEE MEN OF BALLYWOODEN

"It may have been a breath from nowhere," agreed the helper, "so we'll say no more about it."

On flew the curlews till land lay far behind. Then out of the lungs of the ocean came wind. The wee Pilot was on his feet now.

"Stop the music," he ordered, "and every man to his post. First, pull in the curlews and untie the tow-line from their toes. And make sure you don't lose a jot of the farmer's wife's black thread. Hurry, for this is the breeze that'll carry us over the sea. And it's far we may have to sail on a hunt for that Jackdaw."

In less time than a star could wink, the curlews were freed from the Wee Men's ships, and back they flew to the land.

Then the Pilot blew six long blasts on the bullock's horn, and the square sails were set on the wishbone masts. The sails were pitch black, for they had been cut hundreds of years ago out of a black December night. A funnel wind filled the sails, and the Pilot's ship took the lead. In single file the wee ships followed one another, and they sailed away over the rim of the world. And the pilot settled down on the pewit's wing, to look into the compass and watch the wee star flickering in the bubble.

The Musician asked if there was need for more music.

"No," answered the Pilot. "We'll be getting songs now from the moonflakes as they jabble on the waves. Put the blind fiddler's bow away and be sure you don't misplace it, for it's needing it we are, with the bagpipes missing."

The Pilot reached for the bullock's horn and this time blew twelve long blasts. In no time at all the wee Lookout appeared. He was a very old fellow, with a face like a wrinkled boot. He wore a long beard, and this he wrapped around his neck as if it were a muffler, to guard against sea-lane drafts.

"Have you your spyglass handy?" the Pilot asked.

"I have," answered the Lookout, "and ready it is to spy on the world."

"Let me have a look at it," said the Pilot. "We'll have to do some far spying to-night, for come what may, the Jackdaw must be spied upon if we're to find the bagpipes."

The Pilot examined the wee spyglass. "Where did you get this?" he asked. "It looks new."

"Parts of it are," answered the Lookout. "Notice the length of it. A hollow reed it is. I cut it out of

Blaney's Bog. And the part that you look through—there—that's a weazened weazel's eye. And in the other end lies snug and tight a June dewdrop, to magnify."

"Take it, take it," said the Pilot. "It's a magnificent spyglass, so it is. Now up on the main wishbone mast with you and take your stand. Report everything you spy loudly enough so that the ships behind may hear."

Then the Pilot spoke to the crew. "Quit that beard plucking and jumping over one another," he said, "and act like the sailors that you are. And I'll have none of you getting seasick, for we have no time for that. Rest when you can, for any moment you may be needed. Don't forget there's a thieving Jackdaw to be found."

On sailed the ships. The white wakes astern showed the speed they were making. Spray began to fly and wet the decks, and the Wee Men stopped their frolicking and pulled on their oilskin coats.

From aloft came a shout from the Lookout: "I spy a flock of white birds!"

"Is there a black one among them?" called back the Pilot.

"No, no! They're all white!"

"Well, take care and don't let the moon blind you. It's a black bird you're to look out for."

The Keeper-of-the-Potato-Apples, who had the loudest voice among the crew, spoke up. "What shall we do with the Jackdaw when we catch him?" he asked.

"We'll hold a conference and decide," answered the Pilot.

"The thing to do with him," went on the Keeper-of-the-Potato-Apples, "is to put him in a bottle and sink him in Blaney's Bog for a thousand years or more."

"Good! Good!" cried the Pilot. "Pass the word to the ships behind us."

The Keeper-of-the-Potato-Apples pulled his hand away from his mouth, that all the ships might hear. "A thousand years in Blaney's Bog for the thieving Jackdaw!" he roared.

Cheers went up from the ten wee ships. The Pilot called for his pipe. "I must smoke on that," he said, and a Wee Man in a green apron and a white cap brought the Pilot's pipe.

Then the Stirrer-of-the-Gruel appeared and whispered into the Pilot's ear, "The snail is coming out of his shell."

"What!" exclaimed the Pilot. "Don't tell me that!"

The Wee Man in the white cap held out a glow-worm to light the Pilot's pipe.

"No, no," said the Pilot, pushing his pipe away, "I have other things to think about."

The Stirrer-of-the-Gruel, speaking louder now, said, "We'd better reef the sails. There's scud wings on the moon, and that too is a bad sign."

The Pilot took his eye from the compass and called aloft to the Lookout: "What are you spying on now?"

An answer came from the top of the main wishbone mast: "I spy, far, far behind us, the flailers of the deep."

"What are they doing?" reached up the Pilot's voice.

"Beating the waves," roared the Lookout.

The Pilot shook his head, and the sea spray on his beard dropped on the compass. "We're in for something," he said, "when the flailers of the deep appear; that's another bad sign. But come what may, I must keep the wee star gleaming in the bubble."

CHAPTER FIVE

THE PILOT

T HE wee Tinker came running up from the
cabin. Said he to the Pilot: "The worst has happened! The snail is out of his shell and crawling over
the charts."

"Oh! Oh!" cried the Pilot, throwing up his hands,
"we're in for a hurricane!" And no sooner were the
words out of his mouth than the howl of the wind
was heard. And no sooner was the howl heard than

the hurricane was upon them. It struck the wee ships, listing them over with the lee rail under. The wishbone masts squeaked cuckoo noises under the strain. Pretty soon the ships righted themselves and were off before the gale. Then the waves began to rise. There was danger of them tumbling onto the ships.

The Pilot gave a command:

"Hurry, men, and hang the dandelion milk bags over the stern to quiet the waves, or our ships will be smashed into splinters!"

Then a cry came from the Lookout: "I want to come down! I want to come down! I can't hold out any longer! I'm afraid the weasel's eye will be blown through the spyglass."

The Pilot cupped his hands around his mouth and threw back his head. Then up to the top of the mainmast raced his voice. "Don't lose the weasel's eye, or we'll never find the bagpipes! Take a twist with your beard around the top of the mast and stay there!"

As the dandelion milk bags were slung over the ships' sterns, the milk slithered into the open mouths of the waves. There was a guggling sound that the Pilot heard, for he spoke now with more confidence.

"So far, so good," he said. "That has stopped their

tumbling." And he looked behind him to see if all the ships were coming along. There they were, not a cat's tail length away from each other. "Good! Good!" he cried.

Then appeared the Harrower-of-Sea-Ripples, with a harrow in his hand. Said he to the Pilot, "There's water in the hold."

"What!" bellowed the Pilot. "Water in the hold? Don't tell me that. As if I didn't have troubles enough! With a gale and a high sea running, to say nothing of having to steady the wiggle in the compass! And with the scud wings on the moon, it's all I can do to follow the wee star." The Pilot spoke sharply to the Harrower-of-Sea-Ripples. "Don't stand there with your long ears wobbling before my eyes," he said. "Harrow the ripples in the hold, and if that doesn't do any good, call the Red Sand Man to stop the water from seeping through the seams."

The howl of the gale grew louder as it whistled through the masts, and the ships raced away before it, with their black December sails funneled full of wind.

The Gruel Stirrer crawled on hands and knees

across the deck to the Pilot. Said he, "The Wee Men are all shivering from the cold."

"What," said the Pilot, "shivering from the cold? Well, well, never did I have such a night of troubles!"

"Shall I serve them each a clamshell full of gruel?"

"No, no, certainly not," answered the Pilot. "Where do you think you are—in the deep of the cove, sheltered by rocks?"

"But something has to be done," said the Stirrer. "The men have all forgotten their mittens, and their hands are cold and they can't think. You might as well have no crew at all as a crew that can't think. So what are you going to do about it?"

The Pilot thought and thought. Then he pulled a hair out of his head and rolled it between his fingers, wishing the while for an inspiration. And as he rolled the hair, it came. "I have the solution now," he said. "We can't give them gruel, with the spray flying as it is. But rouse up the Bellows Man and have him warm up the crew."

The Bellows Man was called, and he came up out of the cabin with his red flannel shirt open at the neck and his sleeves rolled up. His round puffy cheeks were squeezed between fierce looking eyebrows and a bristling mustache, and when he spoke his voice came in hot gusts.

"There are no crystals in the wind," he said. "Why am I being bothered?"

The Pilot gave him a look that nearly staggered him over the stern. "Another word from you," said he, "and it's back to the bog you'll go. Warm up the crew, and warm them at once, and while you're at it, run aloft and give the Lookout a blast from you, too."

Without another word the Bellows Man went about among the crew, blowing his warm breath on them. And as he went up to each Wee Man, puffing out his cheeks and pursing his lips getting ready to blow, the Wee Man put up his cold hands before his face to get the full force of the warm gust from the Bellows Man. As the crew grew warm again they began to think, and count up on their fingers.

"You may go below again now," said the Pilot to the Bellows Man. "As you pass the snail that's crawling across the charts, give him a blow, too. This hair between my fingers is not twitching for nothing. Blow a blast on the snail, I say."

The crew stared at the Pilot and whispered to one

another, for never before, in their memory, had they
heard of warming up the wee snail.

The Bellows Man ran down to the cabin, and there
he saw, first thing, the glowworm waving its light
over the ink pot that stood beside the charts. And on
one of the charts was the snail, crawling around
slowly, as if it had never a thought of turning back
to its shell. The Bellows Man stooped over close to
the snail, puffed out his cheeks, pursed his lips and
blew such a blast on the snail that it nearly pried him
loose from the chart. But the snail was a ground grip-
per and merely humped its back and pulled in its
horns. The Bellows Man looked puzzled. He shook
himself, swelled out his chest, and made ready to blow
another blast on the snail. Then it was that the snail
straightened itself, stuck out its horns, put its hump
into its crawl, and made for its shell, lickety clip.

The Bellows Man let a gusty laugh out of him, and
as the snail crawled into his shell, he bounded to the
deck to tell the Pilot.

"The snail is back in his shell!" he shouted.

"Of course he is," answered the Pilot. "Nobody
needs to be told that. Isn't that plain enough to be
seen?"

The sea was running smooth, the moon was swimming clear, and the knots were smoothed out of the muscles of the gale.

The Pilot handed the hair that had been twitching between his fingers to the Bellows Man. "Put this away with my other things," he said. "I may need it later to do a bit of thinking."

The Lookout called down from the main wishbone mast: "I see through my spyglass, fish with wings, flying ahead of us!"

"Good!" cried the Pilot. "We're getting somewhere now, for the wee star is sinking in the bubble. If my reckoning is right we're not over sixty shadows of a Wee Man's milestone away from something." Then the Pilot gave a loud command: "Wake up the Meadow Sniffer! I believe we'll be having use for him now."

The Meadow Sniffer came out on deck wearing a primrose cloak. "Do you want me already?" he asked sleepily.

"Yes," answered the Pilot. "Don't you smell something?"

The Meadow Sniffer sniffed through wide nostrils. "I smell pineapples," he announced.

"Bravo!" cried the Pilot. "I expected as much. Are the farmer's horse tails ready?"

The wee Snare Maker spoke up. "They were ready," he said, "before we started."

CHAPTER SIX

THE Pilot spoke to the crew. Said he, "Men, we've weathered the gale, but there's worse than that ahead of us. All of you know the Jackdaw and his tricks. To capture him, will be the test to our wits. But capture him we must, for without our wee bag-pipes there'd be no castle serenades. The snares are ready, so the Snare Maker says, and the Lookout re-

ports there's fish on the wing. And the Meadow
Sniffer's been sniffing pineapples."

At that moment the Stirrer-of-the-Gruel came out
of the galley with a wee blackthorn stick in his hand,
and a thimblefull of gruel showing on his beard. The
Pilot turned from the crew and spoke to him gruffly.

"What have you been doing?"

"Oh, I've been cooking gruel."

"And who ordered you to do that?"

"It's gruel time," answered the Stirrer, "for there's
lug ears in the black December sails."

The Pilot looked up at the sails and then at the
ships behind him.

"You're right," he said. "Serve the gruel. But mind
you, a clamshell of gruel to each man, and no more.
I want my men to be light and empty, for there'll
be more light jumping to-night, if we're to get our
bagpipes back, than there was on the night that the
sea otter made away with the mermaid's comb."

"Don't remind us of that," cried the Snare Maker,
"for never shall I forget that night."

"Nor me; nor me," came shrill voices from the
Wee Men.

The gruel was served, and each man had his whack

—and no more. The crew smacked their lips and clicked their heels together, just to show the Pilot that they were light and springy, and ready to jump over the wishbone masts if he gave the word.

Then all of a sudden a trembling shiver came from the hold of the ship. The Pilot jumped to his feet and crossed his eyes—a sure sign of fright. There was a rippling quiver in his voice.

"Men," he said, "have we run aground? If we have, the jig is up."

The Wee Men all looked scared and began to finger their ears.

"Be calm, men," the Pilot ordered, "if we've struck a rock, we've struck it, but according to my reckoning there's deep-sea water here."

Again came the trembling shiver from the hold. The Gruel Stirrer placed his blackthorn stick behind his ear.

"It's not often I talk," he said, "but when I do, I have something to say. Now if you're in doubt about our being on the rocks, call the wee Diver and send him down to see."

The Pilot uncrossed his eyes and the wriggling wrinkles trailed away from the corners of his mouth.

"I don't know what's the matter with me to-night," he murmured, "but then, I'm never myself after a hurricane." With that he gave an order, and the words came darting out of him: "Rouse up the wee Diver! Hurry men, hurry, before the worst may happen!"

The Bellows Man ran to the cabin and banged on the Diver's door. "Up with you!" he shouted. "And cuff the sleep bleards from your eyes! The ship is on a rock, so the Pilot thinks."

Pulling on his kelpy garments, in a sand-glass second the Diver was on the deck and standing before the Pilot.

"If we're on the rocks," said the Pilot, "I want to know it. There are strange noises below. The like of such were never heard before."

"I thought," answered the Diver, "that something was happening, from the way the grasshopper was acting in the cabin."

"Don't tell me anything I don't know," snapped the Pilot. "Over the side with you and down to the bottom of the sea you go. And mind you, don't get playing around down there with things that don't concern you."

COGGELTY–CURRY

Clay clogs, spiked with lost horseshoe nails, were tied onto the Diver's feet to weigh him down. The Snare Maker then placed a wee clothespin over his nose to keep the water out.

"Now go!" said the Pilot.

So the Diver was dropped over the side of the ship, and down he sank to the bottom of the sea.

The Pilot squinted at the compass, and as he did so, the ship shook from stem to stern.

"If we're not on a rock," spoke up the Stirrer-of-the-Gruel, "then we're on the bulge of the world, and what could be worse?"

"Nothing could be worse," cried the Pilot, "nothing, nothing. Is there any sign from the Diver yet?"

"No," answered the Snare Maker, who was looking over the side. "I see nothing but bubbles—bubbles—bubbles——"

"Well, that's something," said the Pilot; "it shows he's getting somewhere."

A loud call came from the Lookout from the top of the main wishbone mast. "I spy crow clouds ahead! They're as black as a smothered moon!"

Then the Meadow Sniffer cried: "There's rain on the pineapples that I sniff now!"

The Pilot looked displeased. "I wish you'd sniff something else than pineapples," he said. "If you would only get a whiff of the Jackdaw in your nose, now!"

The Snare Maker clapped his hands. "Whist!" he cried. "The Diver is coming to the top, like a wheelbarrow full of daylight. There's something chasing him!"

"What!" exclaimed the Pilot. "Something chasing him?"

"Aye, and his clogs are missing."

The Pilot wrung his hands. "His clay clogs are missing, did you say?"

"Aye, they're gone, but here he is."

The wee Diver jumped on board and the Snare Maker pulled the clothespin off his nose. Then the Diver took a long breath and shook himself as he walked over to the Pilot. Said he, "There are no rocks on the bottom, and the ship sails clear."

The Pilot looked down at the Diver's feet. "So your clay clogs are gone? And the lost horseshoe nails, too?"

"I had a close call," replied the Diver. "I was chased by a sea otter, and he swallowed my clogs."

The Gruel Stirrer spoke up. "What are clogs in a time like this?" he asked. "If that wasn't a rock we struck, what was it?"

The Diver held up his hand for attention. "When I was down in the deeps of the sea," said he, "I placed my ear to the bottom of the ship, and what do you think I heard? The wee Eel, threshing around in the hold."

"Ho, ho!" shouted the Pilot. "So that's what I took for a rock! So that was our own wee Eel! Well, I might have known it. Since the Lookout's been spying crow clouds ahead, and the Meadow Sniffer sniffs rain on his pineapples——"

The Gruel Stirrer took his thorn stick from behind his ear. "What has rain got to do with the Eel and the lost clogs?" he demanded.

The Pilot spoke sharply to the Stirrer-of-the-Gruel. "You must have had more than your share of the gruel to-night, or you wouldn't be blathering the way you do. Don't you know the wee Eel is a fresh-water Eel, and we're sailing into rain? Think of it! Sailing into rain! As if we hadn't had enough to distract us from hunting the thieving Jackdaw!"

The Gruel Stirrer squared his shoulders. "I swear,"

he cried, "by the gruel, the clogs, the rain and the Eel, that if I lay my hands on the Jackdaw, I'll pluck him naked! Aye, and bury the salve that would make his feathers grow again!"

The Pilot nodded grimly as he sat down on the pewit's wing again, and his eyes swung toward the bubble in the compass.

CHAPTER SEVEN

THE wee Well Digger was called to lead the Eel to the deck, for rain had begun to fall and was running down the wishbone masts. The Meadow Sniffer announced that he smelt fire in the crow clouds. "And that's not all," he cried, "for the moon has gone to sleep."

"Enough," said the Pilot, raising his hand, ' the wee star has stopped flickering in the bubble."

THE WEE MEN OF BALLYWOODEN

The Snare Maker cocked his ear to listen. "Whist men," he said, "will you listen to the cloud blacksmith pounding on his anvil?"

"Lights! Lights!" ordered the Pilot. "We must see for ourselves what's going on around here."

The Lamp Trimmer came on deck with a basket full of glowworms. "Where will you have them?" he asked the Pilot.

"String them around the deck, some on the bulwark rails and a couple on the wishbone masts, and one on the flying jib boom. We must not lose sight of the flags. Four of them I want here, to find the wee star."

When the decks were lit up and the Wee Men could see where they were going, the Well Digger stuck his head out of the main hatch and called: "Shall I take the elastic halter off the Eel's neck?"

"You may," answered the Pilot. Then to the crew the Pilot said, "Don't get in his way, men. It's fresh water he's after. That accounts for his threshing around in the hold. The ship couldn't stand much of that—so turn him loose."

"Here he comes!" shouted the Well Digger, and with that the wee Eel crawled over the hatch combings, and skidded onto the wet deck. The crew jumped on top of the galley, but the Stirrer-of-the-Gruel stood with shoulder against the wishbone mast. The Eel glowered around him as if he were getting his bearings. His slanting eyes sought those of the Pilot, and the Pilot politely bowed to him.

"Go on," he said, "and souse yourself. But no more of that tail threshing in the hold. If you had behaved yourself in the past, you might have been one of the crew to-night."

The Eel wiggled his tail angrily and stared at the Gruel Stirrer. The Stirrer-of-the-Gruel stared back at the Eel and spoke to the Pilot.

"He wants more than rain. I know him. If I don't miss my guess, it's a sand-sniper's egg he's after."

"Tut, tut," said the Pilot, "he had his sand-sniper's egg when the rooster crowed, a morning since."

The Eel opened his mouth till it gaped, and raised his head from the deck. "Look out!" shouted the Gruel Stirrer. "He's bringing down a curse on us!"

And at that moment rain that *was* rain came spilling from the clouds. It flooded the decks and doused the crew, and it knocked the wind out of the black December sails.

THE WEE MEN OF BALLYWOODEN

The ship stopped. A dead calm was upon them. Lightning forked around the wishbone masts, and the thunder came louder than an explosion in a wee quarry. Up and down the decks swam the Eel, the mischievous eyes of him glinting in the glowworm light.

The Gruel Stirrer began to wail. "We'll never get back our wee bagpipes if this keeps up! If we had them now, we could play this away and maybe blow a gooseberry leaf full of wind into the sails. But what can we do, with the stars crying, and the blacksmith up there hammering out a rim for the sun?"

"Look!" called the Snare Maker. "The ships behind us have their distress flags up."

"What color are they?" asked the Pilot.

"Buttercup," called back the Snare Maker.

"They're not distress flags," piped up the Stirrer-of-the-Gruel. "They're tear-stained flags, if I know anything."

"Stop your arguing," commanded the Pilot. "This is not the time for flags to be interfering with my thinking. It's a bad time we're having, with the speed of our ships gone, and the sails sleeping, and the Lookout spying nothing. Something must be done, and done at once."

The Pilot dropped his head between his legs. His right hand went up and grabbed the potato-apple tassel on his cap. He squeezed it and squeezed it, and thought and thought. The wee Eel was cutting capers now, waltzing around the rain watered deck with his tail in his mouth.

The Snare Maker spoke to the Well Digger. "Did you ever see such a night?"

"Never," replied the Well Digger. "I've dug many wells, but never did I see water rise like this before. Why, there's no stopping it at all. Unless something is done we'll be floated out of the ships. I'm not a Wee Man that talks very much; I have too much to do. I dig myself a well, and when water comes I call the birds and go off and dig another one. But here we stand, ankle deep, and there the Pilot sits, with his head between his legs, while the Eel is whooping it up. Look at the Sniffer, with not a Sniff in his nose, and there wades the wee Tinker, with a soldering iron in his hand. And the Lookout up there I see is wiping the wet from the weazened weasel's eye. As if that would do any good on such a night as this!"

"Say no more," cried the Snare Maker, "you are shooting shivers through me!"

The Gruel Stirrer stared at the Pilot and shook his head, mumbling the while: "The Jackdaw has nothing to fear from us now. If only I'd put more salt in the gruel, the crews could have lapped all the star tears up."

Just then the Pilot let go of the potato-apple tassel and jumped to his feet. He clicked his squashy heels together, and there was fresh confidence in his command: "Take down all the lights and put them snugly away in their basket."

The Lamp Trimmer hurried, and in no time at all, the glowworms were down and out, and the ships lay as black as the slumbering December sails. The Gruel Stirrer felt for his own nose, and stroked the wee hair on the end of it, saying to himself, "What's the Pilot up to, now?"

He didn't have long to wonder, for he heard a tunneling command:

"Wake up the Sneezer!"

"No, no, no!" came cries from the Wee Men. "Not the Sneezer! Anything but the Sneezer!"

The Pilot took a long breath and held it till a roar

of thunder had rolled away. This time there was no doubt about his order, for his voice sounded like the surf on the sunken reef:

"WAKE UP THE SNEEZER!"

CHAPTER EIGHT

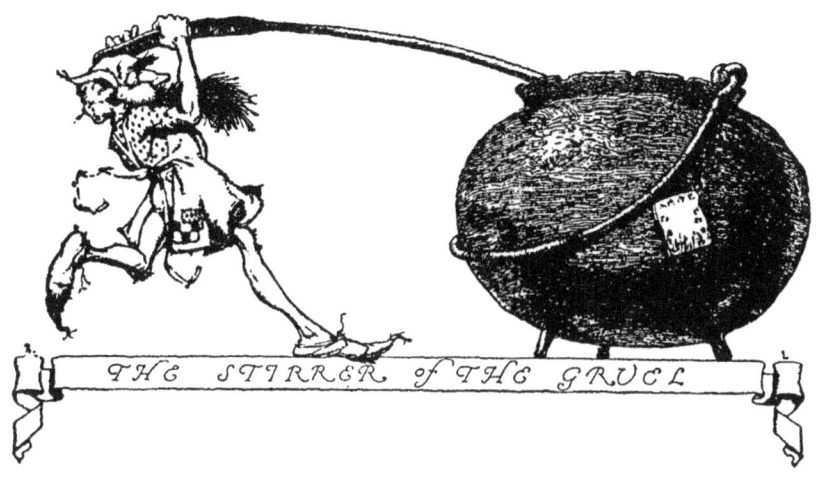

THE STIRRER of THE GRUEL

THE Well Digger took his wee spade out of his hip pocket and made for the cabin. With his spade he knocked on the door of the room next to the pantry.

"Wake up, Sneezer, wake up!" he called. "It's not often you are needed, but the Pilot says you are, to-night. Come, come, no stretching or yawning. There's a light on the ink bottle. You can see to dress."

Pretty soon the door opened and the Sneezer peeped out.

"I suppose," said he, "that things must be in a rather bad way?"

"They are. The worst we've ever encountered."

"Is there any news of the thieving Jackdaw?" asked the Sneezer.

"Not even a smell," answered the Well Digger, sadly.

As the light fell on the Sneezer he looked a beach-flea's leg taller than the Well Digger and much thicker around the chest. His nose was long and his mouth wide. "It won't take me long to clear things up," he said.

"Come on, then," urged the Well Digger. "No bragging. Up to the deck with you."

"Hold on," said the Sneezer. "When I do a job, I have to go prepared for it. Let me see just what I shall wear. Oh, I know, I'll just throw this pink shadow cloak around my shoulders. But there's one more thing I want to know. How hard do you think I'll have to sneeze?"

"That's a hard question to answer," said the Well Digger. "The moon is sick and can't shine, the wee star is not in sight, the ships lie still, the sails hang limp, and the crews can't find an ear to think. And that's not all. If I guess right——"

"No more," said the Sneezer, "or I'll begin to wobble on the job."

With that the Sneezer threw the pink shadow cloak over his shoulders and picked up a tiny box that was labeled, *Sneezing Snooze for Crowding Crow Feathers*. "This will do the work, whatever it may be," said the Sneezer to himself. "It's the most powerful I have."

The Well Digger, followed by the Sneezer, groped his way to the deck. The Sneezer reported to the Pilot. "Well, here I am," said he.

"Oh, I see you," replied the Pilot. "Who wouldn't? Isn't there anything else you could wear besides that pink shadow cloak?"

"I sneeze better in pink," answered the Sneezer.

"Are you ready?"

"I am. Just say the word."

The Pilot spoke to the Stirrer-of-the-Gruel. "Are the crew on top of the galley?"

"Indeed they're not," answered the Gruel Stirrer. "Not one of them do I see."

"Good," said the Pilot. Then he called up to the Lookout: "Hold tight up there!"

"Aye, aye, tight it is," came a wee voice from the top of the main wishbone mast.

The Pilot braced himself. The Gruel Stirrer flung both arms around a wishbone mast. The Well Digger placed his wee spade between his legs and sat down on it, taking a firm hold of the handle. The Sniffer, the Tinker, the Snare Maker, all crouched low on the hatch. The Eel took its tail out of its mouth as it eyed the Sneezer and swam to shelter under the Gruel Stirrer's legs.

The Pilot's loud voice was now heard the length of the ship: "Are we all ready?"

Faint cries came in answer: "We are! We are! But hurry and get it over with!"

"Then sneeze!" commanded the Pilot.

The Sneezer opened his snooze-box and took a heavy pinch between his forefinger and thumb. Then he snuffed the snooze up his long nose. He threw back his head while the Wee Men waited, breathlessly. The Pilot placed his hand over the bubble compass. And then the Sneezer sneezed. The like of such a sneeze had never been heard before. The ship shivered, the jib boom quivered, the wishbone masts buckled, and the sails bulged like the black bottom of the blind fiddler's cockle pot.

The Sneezer was getting ready another sneeze, curling it up in his nose. He spread his legs, and back went his head:

"CHA-WEE-I-SSSH-L——" it came, stronger this time, for the rain stopped falling and the decks were dried. A call came from the Lookout:

"It's clearing ahead! Stop the Sneezer!"

"No, no!" cried the Pilot. "He must sneeze the clothes off the moon."

The Well Digger's wee voice was heard. "We've had enough," he said. "My spade has been sneezed from under me. And the wee Tinker is counting his fingers, and there's one of them missing."

The Pilot would have jumped to his feet and exerted his authority but he dared not, with the Sneezer behind him. As it was, his wee cap had been sneezed away.

A faint moan came from the Gruel Stirrer.

And then the Sneezer sneezed again. This time he made a bright clearing, for the moon and stars came out, and the Milky Way was oozing right across the sky.

The Pilot jumped to his feet and said to the Sneezer: "Bravo! I knew you could do it! It was a hard blow for us all, but we must capture the Jackdaw, and what's a few sneezes, with the wee bagpipes at stake? You've done a good night's work: you've cleared things up and brought the wind. Now go to your cabin and sleep again. I may not need you for another thousand years or more."

The Lookout placed the spyglass to his eye, and as he spied, his heels began to thrum on the wishbone mast. The Wee Men were taking stock of themselves, and no one paid any attention to the thrumming. The Gruel Stirrer claimed there were five and twenty hairs missing from his chin, and three of the thorns were blown off his stick. The Pilot listened to complaints first from one, then from another.

"It was terrible while it lasted," he agreed, "but I'm saying nothing if there is a bare spot on the top of my head. We knew what we were up against when we started this voyage. But now we're off again, with speed on our ships. Don't you feel the wee roll, and the soush of the wind, and the guggling song the

Dolphin scales make? Hurrah! Hurrah! The wee star is back in the bubble again!"

A call came from the Lookout: "I spy an island, far, far away, floating on the rim of the sea!"

"Good!" cried the Pilot. "That'll be the island the Jackdaw is on, for the wee star is pointing that way."

CHAPTER NINE

THE LOOK ~ OUT

THERE was excitement in the Pilot's voice as he
gave his orders. "Put the Eel down in the hold
again."

"Aye, aye," answered the Well Digger. "I have the
elastic halter around his neck now."

"Well, take him out of my sight. I can't bear the
look of him. In a way, he's the cause of a lot of this
trouble."

199

THE WEE MEN OF BALLYWOODEN

The Eel gave the Pilot a slimy stare as he was being led down to the hold. The Gruel Stirrer walked over to the Pilot. Said he:

"This is the worst night I've ever spent on the sea —and I've sailed a bit in my time. I'm not a Wee Man that growls much, but I'd like to know what *are* you going to do with the Jackdaw when you catch him?"

"We've got to capture him first," answered the Pilot, "before we make any further plans. If I know anything about that Jackdaw, it'll be no easy matter. Changing him doesn't seem to make him any better. Now, before I changed him—when he was the player of the wee bagpipes——"

"Oh, don't mention it," interrupted the Gruel Stirrer. "He was a thieving rascal then, too. But to give the likes of him wings—I can't understand it."

"I can't myself," said the Pilot. "But even we make mistakes once in a while."

Then the Gruel Stirrer whispered in the Pilot's ear. "I don't want the crew to hear what I'm saying," said he, "but there's a wee fear that's bothering me."

"Out with it! Out with it!" commanded the Pilot. "This is no time for yarning, with an island ahead, and the night as warm as the farmer's wife's griddle."

The Gruel Stirrer went on whispering in the Pilot's ear, and there was a quiver in his whisper.

The Pilot looked alarmed. "What!" he exclaimed. "Say no more. I never thought of that."

"Hah!" The Gruel Stirrer's whisper grew louder. "And if the Jackdaw dared play it?"

"He couldn't! He hasn't the power," said the Pilot.

"I'm not so sure about that," said the Gruel Stirrer in his natural voice again. "I'm not so sure about what he has, and what he hasn't."

A shout came from the Lookout: "The island grows large! It's five and fifty hunted hare-jumps across. I spy palm trees, and low-lying huts."

"What else are you spying?" called up the Pilot.

"A long lagoon, and a white sandy beach, and coconut trees——"

"That's not enough," shouted the Pilot. "You should be spying more, according to my calculations."

The Lookout thrummed his feet violently on the wishbone mast. Then the Gruel Stirrer spoke, that all might hear. Said he, "My left foot itches."

"Bravo!" cried the Pilot. "That's a good sign; the best yet."

Again came a shout from the Lookout, this time a frightened one. "I spy an army of wee mountains! They're moving, and carrying their huts on their backs! They're digging holes in the sand with their hind legs!"

Everyone shivered with fear, but the Pilot reached for the pewit's wing and fanned himself.

"Men," he said, "shake the shivers out of yourselves. It's just like the Jackdaw, to pick an island like this, with wee moving mountains digging holes in the sand. But swallow your fears. Get into your jumping clogs and be ready to land. For with the speed that we're going, we'll be there in an echo's time."

As the ten wee ships sailed up the lagoon, the Lookout's voice once more reached down: "This is the island the Jackdaw is on, for the weazen has left the weasel's eye."

"That's what I've been waiting to hear," said the Pilot. "The weazen doesn't leave the weasel's eye for nothing—not if I know weasels."

"You'll not be needing me," said the Stirrer-of-

Closer and closer sailed the wee ships toward the coconut trees.

the-Gruel, "to hunt the Jackdaw. My job is to stir the gruel."

"You're going ashore with the rest," answered the Pilot, "and every Wee Man of you carries a handful of snares from the farmer's horses' tails. Don't be talking to me now. Can't you see I'm landing the ships?"

Closer and closer sailed the wee ships toward the coconut trees. The Wee Men all had their jumping clogs on and laced tight to their feet. All but the Stirrer-of-the-Gruel. He looked scared, and well he might, for on the beach, not a cable length away, were many many turtles laying their eggs in the sand. Never had the Wee Men seen such a sight as this before.

The Gruel Stirrer stood up before the Pilot. Said he, "The wee mountains are moving, and my advice is not to land with the like of them digging in the sand. After all, we have to look out for ourselves. Suppose they're a new kind of wee folk? They wouldn't be out this time of night unless they were something like us. I'm telling you now, so I'll have my say over; don't count on me to help snare the Jackdaw."

THE WEE MEN OF BALLYWOODEN

The Pilot gave the Gruel Stirrer a look that showed the whites of his eyes. "Another word from you," he said, "and I may change you into something you won't like."

The Stirrer-of-the-Gruel stamped on the deck with his blackthorn stick. "You haven't the power," he said, "for if you did, you'd drive those wee moving mountains away."

The Pilot scratched the bald spot that the Sneezer had given him on the top of his head, and he gave a quick command: "Lower the sails down!" he roared.

Each ship sailed up to a coconut tree and was tied fast with a stout rope that had been twisted out of the whine of a wintry wind. The Pilot looked at the turtles in the sand. His Wee Men must get past them some way or other; but how? That was the thing that puzzled him. He thought and thought, and as he was doing his best thinking, the Gruel Stirrer interrupted him.

"Don't figure me in your thinking," he said, "for not a move shall I make to hunt the Jackdaw. I'm not only the Stirrer-of-the-Gruel, but I pass your orders from ship to ship."

At that moment the Lookout gave a call down the wishbone mast.

"Whist! Whist!" He held up his spyglass for silence.

And then to the ears of the Wee Men came far-away notes from their own wee bagpipes.

"Men," said the Pilot, "courage is what we need now. You're all hearing the Jackdaw playing the bagpipes?"

The Gruel Stirrer interrupted again. "Look! Look!" he cried. "The wee moving mountains are listening, too!"

And sure enough, the turtles had stopped laying eggs in the sand to listen to the tune from the wee bagpipes.

"Get into your jumping clogs," said the Pilot to the Gruel Stirrer. "I've put up with a lot from you, to-night. It's plain to me now, you've had more gruel than is good for you. Don't think, just because you have a loud voice, that you can interrupt whenever you want to and have things arranged to suit you. It's only once in a lifetime anyway that you say any thing worth listening to. Get into your clogs! The wee men are waiting, with snares in their hands."

The Stirrer-of-the-Gruel squared his wee shoulders and stroked the lone hair on the end of his nose. Said he, "You all know me. I'm the Stirrer-of-the-Gruel, and my place is on the ship, to keep the gruel hot."

The Wee Men looked at the Pilot, for never before had anyone dared to speak to him like this. The Pilot's eyes began to roll as he stared at the Stirrer. The Wee Men drew back, feeling sure that something was going to happen.

Then the Pilot spoke, and there was a dungeon roar in his voice. "I have asked you twice to get into your jumping clogs. I'll ask you again, but no more."

"You're wasting your time," said the Stirrer-of-the-Gruel. "Go on with the hunt. Look at the moon slithering over the sky. The first thing you know there'll be shadows, and then where will you be?"

The Pilot began to spin like a top around the Stirrer, and as he did so, strange sounds came out of him. The Wee Men crouched low on the deck, but the Stirrer stood his ground defiantly, with his eyes riveted on the moon.

Faster and faster spun the Pilot; then all of a sudden he stopped and spoke just one word. And the word he said was:

"BEAVER!"

Instantly the Stirrer-of-the-Gruel was turned into a wee beaver.

CHAPTER TEN

THERE was not a whimper out of the Wee Men till the Pilot got his breath. Then the Well Digger whispered to the Snare Maker. "I didn't know that he had as much power as all that. Not with the Gruel Stirrer, anyway."

"Hush! Hush!" The Snare Maker shook his head. "Not so loud. Wait till he cools off, and see what he does next."

Gradually the white left the Pilot's eyes and his wee chest stopped humping. "Men," he said, "straighten yourselves up and get the feel of your clogs. There's nothing to fear now." He looked at the Beaver. "Ashore with you," he commanded, "and scatter those wee moving mountains away."

The Beaver slammed the deck with his broad tail and stared at the Pilot. Then the Pilot stamped three times on the deck with his right foot. At that the Beaver bowed, and over the rail he jumped, and onto the sandy beach.

Up among the big turtles he ran, sniffing in their egg holes. The turtles were badly frightened at the sight of a beaver, and especially this one, and in no time at all the Beaver had scared them all away. Back to the water they ran, like a humping wave.

"Bravo!" cried the Pilot. "Now, every one of you land, with your snares in your hands. Not you," he called up to the Lookout, "you stay where you are and peep on proceedings."

Then the Wee Men from the ten wee ships jumped

onto the sand. The Pilot whistled to the Beaver. "Come here, you," he said, "and leave those big white eggs alone."

The Beaver came running to the Pilot's feet. Never was there such an obedient beaver.

The Pilot looked over his men. Said he, "Are you all ready?"

"We are," they answered.

"Is Split Ear the Glue Man here?"

"That I am," piped up the Glue Man. "Here's my brush and pot of glue, and what I stick stays stuck. My glue is made from the rose marrow of rainbow legs."

"Good," said the Pilot. "That's the stuff that sticks. If the Jackdaw can be made to light on that glue—— But come, away with you all, to where you hear the notes from the wee bagpipes. Remember, no noise, not even a whisper! And don't let me hear or see one of you trying the jumping springs in your clogs before I give the order. Ready! March!"

The Pilot and the Beaver took the lead. The Snare Maker and Sniffer came next, and the Well Digger marched with the wee Tinker. Split Ear the Glue Man followed with the Keeper-of-the-Potato-Apples.

Then followed all the rest of the crews. Every man of them carried a horse-tail-hair snare.

Across the sandy beach they marched and in among the trees. A wisp of a whisper came from the Well Digger. "Suppose the night should open its eye?"

"Hush!" came from the wee Tinker. "Not so loud. We're getting close to the Jackdaw. Do you hear the tune he's playing?"

"Aye, that I do. It sounds a bit like the barn banshee."

Again the wee Tinker warned the Well Digger. "Hush! Not so loud. The Pilot's ears are turning red, and he's squinting around."

Through the palms and coconut trees the Wee Men streamed. Louder and louder came the music from the wee bagpipes. The Pilot stopped and beckoned his Wee Men around him. Said he, in a thistledown whisper, "We're almost upon the Jackdaw. A wrong move now, and things may go bad for us."

The moment the Pilot took his eyes off the Beaver he began to run here and there, gathering little sticks. All at once the Pilot spotted him. "None of that," he called in a whip-like whisper. "You'll build no dams here—not if I know it. Behave yourself and come here."

The Beaver obeyed.

"Now then, men," the Pilot motioned them on, "we'll creep up on the Jackdaw. Use your short breaths. Don't socket your eyes nor trail your long beards, for the least bit of noise may scare the Jackdaw. If he takes to the wing, it'll be hard on the springs of your wee jumping clogs."

"If we could scare the Jackdaw," whispered the Well Digger, "he might drop the bagpipes."

"Hush," said the Pilot, "you don't know him at all. It's a scare that he wants, to get his heart back again to where it belongs."

"What!" came wee whispers.

"Aye, well you may ask. A long time ago—oh, he was well behaved,. then—a plucker of dewdrops from midsummer morns—somehow or other he fell slantwise, from reaching, and down he came scooning on a big gander's back. He was scared so badly that his heart jumped to the right side of his breast. So now you know how he'd welcome a scare. But no more of this whispering. Every one of you down on your fours and creep."

THE WEE MEN OF BALLYWOODEN

Then on they went, on hands and knees. The Pilot took the lead, with the Beaver creeping by his side.

Ahead of them, not fifty crane strides away, stood a swaying palm tree, and there, lying on his back, on a wide spreading palm, was the Jackdaw, blowing the bagpipes. His body swayed in rhythm as his right wing pumped the wee bellows. With his claw feet he played on the reed chanter. He was in fine tune and enjoying himself, for he had an admiring audience. Surrounded he was by all the parrots of the island and love birds, too. For never had they heard such wonderful music. They cocked their ears to hear every note and flapped their wings in appreciation. This pleased the Jackdaw, for he swelled his chest and played all the louder. So entranced was he with his own performance that he never heard the Wee Men creep up to the tall palm tree. Around it they crept, and, lying flat on the ground, they waited for orders from the Pilot. The Pilot sat down on his hunkers and dusted his beard. He'd been trailing dead leaves, and the noise that he made as he shook them out of his beard scared the parrots and love birds away.

All of a sudden the Jackdaw stopped playing, turned up on his feet, but still holding the bagpipes, he peered all around him. Then he hopped to the edge of the palm branch and stared down—right into the eyes of the Pilot.

"Ho, ho!" cried the Jackdaw, "so there you are, down there, and the Wee Men with you! Well, it's not so bad as I thought. I was afraid it was my bad playing had scared my listeners away."

The Pilot sprang to his feet. His eyes flashed an order to his men: "Up and at him!"

"Hold on," said the Jackdaw. "I wish you'd tell me what you're here for—with the whole clan of Wee Men. What have *I* done now?"

"What have *you* done?" roared the Pilot. "You've stolen the bagpipes, bad luck to your quills!" The Pilot shook his fist at the thief. "When I lay hands on you, your days of swinging wings are over!"

"Oh, is that so?" said the Jackdaw, ruffling his breast feathers. "We'll see about that. But first answer me a question. There's something familiar about that Beaver. Who was he before to-night?"

Before the Pilot could answer, the Well Digger spoke up.

"He was the Stirrer-of-the-Gruel."

"Poor old Stirrer," chuckled the Jackdaw. "And

look at him now, showing his teeth, as mad as the Pilot. He and I were the wasp chasers once. You wouldn't think that, to look at him now."

The wily Jackdaw was talking in order to delay the workings of the Pilot's mind, as well as to give himself time to collect his own wits.

He really was a bit frightened, but not enough to flutter his heart back to where it belonged. If he were caught, there was no knowing what the pilot might change him into—he had been changed so many times. And he had a great fear—that of being changed into a worm—bait for catching fry. Nothing would be more humiliating, and the thought of it made the pin feathers friz up on his breast. But he spoke up pertly to the Pilot.

"Who'll be at home to beat the drum when the cock crows?"

"I'm not here to answer your questions," said the Pilot. "Come down here out of that tree and hand over the wee bagpipes, peacefully."

"Oh, no," answered the Jackdaw. "I didn't fly all this distance just for the fun of it. I'm not going back. I'm here to play on the bagpipes, and besides, I have a bit of power that I gathered on this flight."

"He's just bluffing," said the Snare Maker. "He hasn't any power or he'd have used it long ago. But we'd better hurry and catch him, for I hear the far-away rumble of the morn."

"Tut, tut," said the Tinker, "it's the Beaver's heart you hear thumping."

The Pilot fixed his eye on the Jackdaw and gave three quick winks.

The Jackdaw laughed. "I told you I had power, didn't I? You can't blink me off this palm—nor catch me, either."

The Pilot looked puzzled. Were his winks out of order?

"Men," he said, "get ready to jump. I'll say to the Jackdaw again: Come out of that tree and hand over the bagpipes. Remember, your punishment will be less if you do."

"Oh, is that so?" sneered the Jackdaw. "But tell me, how was the blind fiddler's boy when you left? I'm wondering if he got the message I hung on the weather vane of the farmer's house. I doubt if he did. I left word to put the blind fiddler's bow into a crock of buttermilk."

The Pilot began to scratch on the ground with his feet.

"Now," he cried, "nothing will save you! Hanging messages on weather vanes for the blind fiddler's boy to read!"

CHAPTER ELEVEN

S PLIT–EAR," called the Pilot, "start sticking
your glue. Smear it everywhere—any place the
Jackdaw could light on. We'll get him now! Think
of it! The news of the Wee Men he's been spreading
around!"

"Oho," said the Jackdaw. "So you brought Split
Ear along to stick me to trees?"

"Aye," replied the Pilot, "and the wee Tinker's
here, too, to solder your wings."

"Haw-haw!" laughed the Jackdaw. "I think I'll use *my* power and change all the parrots into wee tree men. I'll leave their beaks on, and I can tell you they have a bite you'll remember."

The Well Digger nudged the Pilot. "Be careful," he whispered. "If he can change the parrots and leave their beaks on, why, every man of us would be chased off the island."

"You're talking nonsense," said the Pilot. "I know the Jackdaw, and I've had enough of his bluffing. I have given him his last chance to hand over the bagpipes. Now we'll use force and bring him to time."

With that the Pilot stuck out his wee chest and gave a command.

"Set your snares, men, but be careful of Split Ear's glue. You can jump to the high limbs with the wee springs in your clogs. Tie your snares tight and leave a wide loop for the Jackdaw's feet. Away with you!"

The Wee Men spread themselves out, and each took a tree. Then the jumping began. The horse-tail-hair snares, with their slipknot loops, were clove-hitched to the limbs of the trees.

The Jackdaw spread his tail and sat down on it.

228

Said he, calling down to the Pilot, "I've never seen such poor jumping before. Tell me, what springs did you take those springs out of, for their wee jumping clogs?"

The Pilot spoke gruffly. "You'll have the chance before long to ask the Well Digger that question."

"Don't be too sure of that," answered the Jackdaw. "I'm sitting high on this palm, and a mountain spring couldn't reach me. And if Split Ear should take it into his head to climb this tree—well, I'm warning you—I'll stick him with his own glue. And what's more—I'll nibble his split ears clean off of his head."

The Pilot staggered with anger and fell over the Beaver. But when he picked himself up, he began to think. All of a sudden he stuck his thumb in his ear and whistled low, a sure sign of a worth-while thought. He spread his legs and pulled his thumb out of his ear and stared at the Beaver.

The Snare Maker walked up to the Pilot. Said he, "The snares are all set; some of them high, some of them low. The Well Digger seems to jump higher than any, to-night."

"That's to be expected," answered the Pilot.

Then Split Ear the Glue Man came waddling along with his pot in his hand.

"Is your job well done?" the Pilot asked.

"It is that," answered Split Ear. "There isn't a leaf or a palm on the island that hasn't got its glue—with the exception of the one the Jackdaw is roosting in. But just say the word and I'll climb this tree and finish the job completely."

"No, no," said the Pilot. "I'll not have you glue this tree. The risk is too great, entirely."

The Well Digger came hurrying in jumps to the Pilot. He spoke with a shiver of fear in his voice. "Who is going to mow the mist off the bog in the morning?"

The Pilot answered him sharply. "We have other things to think about now, and besides, the bog has never been missed a morning since I can remember."

The Jackdaw, who had been listening, got up from off his tail feathers to have a word to say. "If the bog mist isn't mown," said he, "the farmer's goats will go astray, and then where will you get your milk?"

The Well Digger nudged the Pilot. "That's something to think about," he said.

CHAPTER TWELVE

THE Jackdaw was beginning to feel a bit uneasy as all the wee snare setters circled his tree. He could hear their whisperings, but he was unable to catch a word of what they were saying. He felt sure that there was not a Wee Man among them who would dare climb to the height where he sat. They were afraid of his claws and a bang from the bagpipes. They were scheming below him; he was certain of that. The glue he could smell, and the snares were all set.

The Pilot spoke, that all might hear. "Men, get out of harm's way, for the Beaver is going to cut down this tree, and I don't want a flying chip to bruise your bodies or blacken your eyes."

The Wee Men backed away as the Beaver's teeth hacked in on the tree. Then it was that the Jackdaw preened his feathers, ready for flight. But where might he light? Could he wing long enough to wear the Wee Men out? He looked up at the moon, and his heart fluttered. If only he'd thought of it and brought a wee bag of daylight along to scatter over the island. He knew well the Pilot's great fear—a bit of misplaced daylight. The blind fiddler's boy was to blame for all this. If he'd put the bow in the buttermilk all would have been well.

As the Beaver's chips started flying, the tree began to rock.

"Good work!" the Pilot cried. "Good work! You're into the heart of it now. And men, a word of warning before it falls. Don't lose your heads, and have a care where you chase when the Jackdaw takes to wing. And above all, don't get stuck in Split Ear's glue."

The wee Tinker tapped the Pilot on the shoulder. Said he, "I've never seen such strength in a Beaver."

"That's nothing to wonder at," said the Pilot. "He's been having more than his share of gruel for the last few hundred years."

"You'll be keeping him as he is?" asked the wee Tinker.

At that moment a shout came from the Meadow Sniffer: "Look out, men, the tree is leaning, and the Jackdaw is trying his wings."

"Good!" cried the Pilot. "Everything is working as I expected."

Then down came the palm tree with a terrible crash, and away flew the Jackdaw. Cheers went up from the Wee Men.

"Hush!" commanded the Pilot. "What do you think you're doing? Wheeling sunset out of the caves? Have a care, and don't let this night's work go to your heads. Did the Jackdaw, by any chance, leave the wee bagpipes behind him?"

"He did not." There was a gravel rattle in the Well

Digger's voice. "Not he. He took them along. There he goes now, winging over our heads."

"I see him," said the Pilot. "He's tantalizing me. He'll soon tire out, and then he'll have to alight, for he can't lug the wee bagpipes for the rest of the night."

"And when he does light," spoke up Split Ear, "he'll stick to my glue."

"Oh, I don't know about that," said the Snare Maker.

"Now, now," interrupted the Pilot, "no arguing. Who cares what catches him, so long as he's caught?"

"The snares have their chance," said the Snare Maker.

"Of course, of course," answered the Pilot.

"The snare may be a help," said Split Ear, "but my glue is the glue that holds."

The Pilot jumped up on the butt of the tree. "If I hear any more arguing," he said, "I may change one of you into a bow-and-arrow man, to shoot the Jackdaw down."

"That's a fine idea," said the wee Tinker.

The Keeper-of-Potato-Apples voiced his opinion.

"I've known the jackdaw when he was a well behaved Wee Man,"
said the Meadow Sniffer.

"Don't use an arrow on the Jackdaw. You might puncture the bagpipes."

"That's to be considered," said the Pilot, thoughtfully.

"I don't care what happens," said Split Ear, "but I know what's in my glue."

The Pilot gave Split Ear a stare. "You're doing too much bragging. How about that bridge you stuck over Guttery Gap?"

"Look!" cried the Well Digger. "Look at the Jackdaw! He's fighting with himself, up there!"

The Pilot placed his hands on his hips and threw his head back. And as he gazed upward, he spoke. "That's some new trick he's playing on me. But it won't work. He's got to alight, sooner or later."

The Jackdaw had been circling over the fallen tree, apparently looking for a place to alight. Now he stopped circling, and balancing himself with his wings, he began to scold. The language that he used made the Wee Men's breath come in jerks. The Meadow Sniffer pulled his primrose cloak around his shoulders.

"I've known the Jackdaw when he was a well behaved Wee Man," said he. "He's been stung by bees and mired in the bog, but never did I hear him use such language."

"Keep quiet," ordered the Pilot. "If I calculate right, there's a strange power working on him. I'd like to know what it is, for it's not coming from me. I thought maybe he was tricking, but I see I'm mistaken. We're on a strange island. We're new to this place."

It did seem that the Jackdaw was being pulled by some power. He began to fly slowly, as if being hauled on a string.

The Well Digger pinched the Pilot's leg. "Have you a bite of a thorn apple on you?" he asked. "There's fear in my feet, and my skin's shriveling up. We're in the hands of a power we know nothing about. Look at the Jackdaw and the fight he puts up. Oh, it was a terrible mistake to come on this voyage!"

The Pilot shivered. "Say no more," he groaned. "Here's the thorn apple to warm your feet."

The Wee Men covered their eyes with their hands when they saw the Jackdaw viciously pluck the blackest feathers out of his breast to shield him from the power that was pulling him on. He was high

242

above the trees now, and reluctantly flying in one direction.

"Uncover your eyes," the Pilot called to his men. "We can only wait and see what the power may be. And if the worst comes, I'll sprinkle you all with salt, or better still, dust you with powdered nettle leaves. No power that I know of could touch you then."

"That may be all right," wailed the wee Tinker, "but that's not getting our bagpipes. We'll never get them now." And the Tinker began to cry, and all the Wee Men cried, and the Pilot, too. The only dry eyes were those of the Beaver. He flopped his broad tail and grinned at the Pilot.

The Keeper-of-the-Potato-Apples, who wept more than any, spoke up. "The Jackdaw has disappeared entirely," said he.

"Stand still, all of you!" commanded the Pilot. "Stop your crying, or you'll be making a lake and maybe get mired in your own tears. Gather around me and lie close to the ground. This new power has upset some of my calculations."

"What's troubling me most," whined the Well

Digger, "is that the snares and the glue mean nothing at all."

"Silence!" said the Pilot. "Haven't we troubles enough without borrowing more? Sink your teeth in your tongues, for I'm doing a bit of thin thinking."

CHAPTER THIRTEEN

WHEN the Jackdaw flew off the falling tree
he thought he'd play a trick on the Wee Men.
It was to circle, and circle, and circle around, and
make every man of them dizzy. He figured that if
they started chasing him all over the island he might
lose his head and light on a sticky tree, where snares
and glue were set to catch him. And at first he circled boldly, with not a thought of fear. Then sud-

denly he grew conscious of a wicked eye pulling him straight. Try as he would, he could not fly away from that check-rein stare. He fought for a while with big heavy words, trying to break the spell, but that eye tugged him on, with the strength of the ropes that moored the wee ships. As he felt himself being drawn, he made one last attempt to free himself. Plucking the blackest feathers from his breast, he tried to make a screen to hide behind. But for all that, he felt himself being pulled only the faster. There was nothing to keep him from being drawn straight to that eye-pulling power.

High on the cuckoo wishbone mast sat the Lookout, with a smile on his wee face and his spyglass pointed in front of him, spying on the Jackdaw. As the Jackdaw flew off the palm tree, the Lookout noticed that the weasel's eye in the spyglass was acting queerly. It began to wink, and wink, and wink, and not only that, but the eye was growing larger, and there was danger of it bursting the end of the spyglass and maybe getting away.

The Lookout was beside himself. He didn't know what to do. The Pilot was away on the hunt, the Sneezer was asleep, and the Eel in the hold was of no use at all. He tried to peer through the spyglass to see how things were going, but the weasel's eye was so magnetic that it nearly stabbed his own. So he pointed the spyglass in front of him, and pretty soon a wee smile crept into his face. For he saw the Jackdaw, coming straight toward the weasel's eye. Closer and closer flew the Jackdaw, still carrying the wee bag-pipes. As he came close, the Lookout saw not only that, but the bald spot on his breast as well, and what he heard the Jackdaw saying, he didn't wish to re-member.

And then it happened. The Jackdaw flew right to the end of the spyglass and there he stuck, with a fas-cinated eye.

The Lookout tried to pull him away, but he couldn't budge him, nor could he pull the wee bag-pipes out of his claws.

He thought and thought what he should do. It was a ticklish time, with no council at hand. If the wink should leave the weasel's eye, the Jackdaw might fly away again.

The Lookout took a firm grip on the spyglass, and he said to the Jackdaw, "I'm going down the mast. Are you coming?"

"There's no help for me," panted the Jackdaw, "unless you blink the wink out of the weasel's eye."

"I can't do that," answered the Lookout. "I take orders from the Pilot." And with that the Lookout slid down the mast, followed by the Jackdaw on the end of the spyglass.

The Lookout picked up the bullock's horn and blew three quick blasts. The Pilot heard it and roared a command: "Get to your feet, men, and run to the ships! Something has happened. If our ships are adrift by a trick of the Jackdaw—well, I still have a bit of power left."

"If you have," cried the Well Digger, "you'd better be using it, for look at the moon. She is mashing yellow turnips up there. You know she begins work before the limpet opens its eyes."

"Run!" roared the Pilot. "Run! No arguments now. There's a sea of time left. Go, do all that I ask of you."

As the Wee Men climbed aboard the bullock horn ship, a cheer went up from all. Even the Pilot gave vent to his feelings and fanned himself with the pewit's wing. There stood the Lookout with the spyglass in his hand, and clinging by an eye to the end of it was the Jackdaw, and in his claws were the wee bagpipes.

The Pilot took command. "Silence!" he ordered. "You've cheered enough for a night. I knew the power of that weasel's eye, for I bottled it a thousand years ago, and fortunately the Lookout dug it up. Now, away with you, men, and gather up your snares. Don't bother about the glue, for there will be a rainbow in the morning. I'll attend to the Jackdaw and be ready for sailing before you return. I'm warning you to hurry, for our ships must be in the cove before the rooster crows."

As the Wee Men ran away for their snares, the Beaver sniffed the Jackdaw.

"Get back there!" ordered the Pilot. "What do you know about weasels' eyes? You're always butting in and gabbling about things that don't concern you."

The Pilot took hold of the Jackdaw. "Come here," he said. "What I won't do to you! Give me the bagpipes."

But the Jackdaw couldn't let go of the bagpipes, nor could the Pilot pull him away from the end of the spyglass.

"Oh!" exclaimed the Pilot. "I might have known this. The weasel's eye is magnetized."

"What are you going to do?" asked the Lookout. "I have a lame shoulder from holding him up."

"Do?" said the Pilot. "Do you think I'm without power? Tut, tut, man. Give me the spyglass. You hold the Jackdaw. But mind that you hold him. From the sound of the susk of the sea on the reefs, it's time we were away."

The Pilot opened a small bag, one of many, that hung around his neck, and out of it he took a pinch of goldenrod pollen. This he dropped into the weasel's eye. Instantly the Jackdaw and bagpipes were loose.

"Hold him tight," said the Pilot. "Don't let him go. I have use for the blackguard. I'm not saying what."

The Pilot laid the spyglass on the combings of the hatch. "Hand me the bagpipes," he said to the Lookout. "I feel a thought coming, and I think it's one of many. It will be a quick way of going home."

"Don't squeeze me so tight!" cried the Jackdaw. "I don't care what happens to me now—anything but a weasel's eye."

The Wee Men were running back to their ships with their snares in their hands.

"Have you gathered them all?" asked the Pilot.

"I saw to that," answered Split Ear. "If I hadn't gone along, every man of them would have been stuck to my glue."

"Get the glue out of your head," said the Pilot. "Think of something else. Where's the Musician?"

"Here I am," piped he.

"Here, take the bagpipes. But don't start a tune till you get an order from me, for I'm doing some deep-sea thinking."

The Pilot lay down with his ear to the deck, while the Wee Men crowded around. Never had they seen the Pilot doing his thinking this way before.

Pretty soon he jumped to his feet and blew a long blast from the bullock's horn. As the echo rode away, he spoke. "Men," said he, "board your own ships. We're ready to sail. Make tow ropes out of your mooring lines and tow one behind the other."

"Towing?" questioned the Well Digger. "With the razor fish peeping out of the sand, and the mountain beyond, with smoke coming out of it?"

The Pilot stamped his foot. "If you open your

mouth again," he said angrily, "and a word floats out of it, I'll sink you where you are, with Whang the Miller's grinding stone around your neck. And let this be a warning to all of you. Now then, let go your lines from the coconut trees! Are you all ready?"

"We are! We are!" came wee jolly voices.

The Pilot took the Jackdaw out of the Lookout's hands and called for the farmer's wife's spools of black thread. Up to the forecastle head he moved, and there he began to spin like a top. Faster and faster he spun. The wee Tinker whispered to the Meadow Sniffer, "Don't look at him. He may twist the moonlight away from your eyes."

All of a sudden the Pilot stopped spinning and shouted one word:

"BARRACOUTA!"

At the same instant he dropped the Jackdaw, and in his place appeared a big fish with raking teeth, that flopped around on the forecastle head.

In no time at all, the Pilot made a tow rope out of the black spool thread and tied the end securely around the dorsal fin of the Barracouta.

"Into the sea with you!" commanded the Pilot, "and home to our coves you tow us!"

The Barracouta plunged over the bows. Straight ahead he swam. The Pilot paid out the towline until he thought it was enough. Then he tied the end around the wee capstan and aft he ran to the bullock's horn. He was just about to blow it when the Barracouta took a sheer. There came a grating noise. The ship was on a reef.

The Pilot staggered into the arms of the Well Digger.

"Oh, oh," he groaned, "I forgot to change the Jackdaw's tricks, and now we're on the rocks!"

He straighened up and shook the dew from off his eyebrows.

The Well Digger shrugged his shoulders and whispered to the Sniffer. "If I were allowed to talk, I'd say something that would turn the Pilot blue. Here we are, stuck on a rib of the ocean. Things are going from bad to worse. I'm not a Wee Man that hankers after trouble, but the Pilot, when he changes things, ought to change tricks, too. Now look at the Barracouta, with the head of him high out of the water, looking back at us with a grin on his mouth. And there stands the Pilot, with thoughts flying out of him, and what do they amount to?"

The Pilot began to pace the deck. Said he, "Every man of you stop your thinking and leave this job to me."

Up and down the deck he paced, thinking all the while. Then suddenly he stopped in front of the Musician. "Can you play us a tune," he asked, "that'll rake us off this reef?"

The Musician looked dubious. "I'll try," he said. "I'll play all the rock tunes I know."

He began to play on the bagpipes, first one tune and then another, but never a move did the ship make.

"Stop!" ordered the Pilot. "You're doing more harm than good. You're only choking time. I know there's a tune in the bagpipes for scraping barnacles off barge bottoms, but I don't know the name of it."

The Musician shook his head. "Nor I, either," he said.

The Beaver began to run around in a circle. "What!" exclaimed the Pilot. "Does he know something?"

The Harrower-of-Ripples appeared from nowhere. "My job takes most of my time," said he. "It's seldom I'm not pulling my harrow, but to-night the breaths are sleeping. Now that our ship lies on the reef I've come to tell you that the Beaver there is the only one among us who can pull us off the rocks."

With that the Harrower disappeared. The Pilot stared at the Beaver. "I might have known," he said, "since you are the oldest one of the lot."

The Beaver stopped running around and lay down at the Pilot's feet. Then the Pilot spoke pleasantly.

"Men," he said, "I'm going to make another change, somewhat against my will, but the Harrower thinks it's for the best. So stand back, all of you, while I make the change."

The Pilot began to spin, and never had he spun so fast before. The red heels of his boots came together with a click as he stopped.

He spoke: "STIRRER-OF-GRUEL!"

Instantly, there stood the Stirrer. The first thing he did was to feel of his teeth. "What have I been eating?" he asked, "Not gruel, I'm sure."

The wee Tinker shook him by the hand. "Glad to see you again," he said. "I'll be telling you all about your teeth and the chewing you've been doing, when I'm mending your pots."

THE WEE MEN OF BALLYWOODEN

The Pilot handed the Stirrer the bagpipes. Said he, "Do you know the tune that scrapes barnacles off barge bottoms?"

"That I do, and well," answered the Stirrer-of-the-Gruel. "It's an old, old tune called, 'Coggelty-Curry.' Just give me room to swing in while I play it."

At the first few notes the ship began to squeak, as if the bottom were being torn out of her. Then came jolly, skipping notes, that almost skipped the Wee Men off their feet. Around and around the deck the Stirrer swung, with his head thrown back and his chest thrown out. Louder he piped, and Coggelty-Curry filled the air.

Then something happened. The Barracouta's head went under and his tail began to wiggle. The Pilot ran to the bubble compass.

"We're off!" he shouted. "Now we're on the way home to our coves."

The Gruel Stirrer stopped playing, and glad enough the Wee Men were, for never had they heard such a tugging tune before.

"Here, take your bagpipes," said the Stirrer to the Pilot. "I'm going to the galley to cook a pot of gruel."

"Good," said the Pilot, "but don't forget our share of the gruel."

"No, nor mine either," said the Stirrer as he winked at the wee Tinker.

THE farmer's rooster jumped down off the roost
and flopped his wings. Then he crowed three
times.

"Get up, John," called the farmer's wife. "There's
a new day here."

"Yes, yes; it's up I am," he answered, "and lacing
my boots."

"And, John, put the porridge on, as you go to the
stable."

"To be sure, to be sure. Don't I always do that?"

As the farmer opened the stable door, he saw that his horses were eating their oats.

"Well, well," said he, "how did this come about, and me asleep in my bed all the night?"

He spoke to the big black mare. "Move your rump over," he said.

And as she did, she slapped him in the face with a full tail of hair. He looked at the other horse. Sure enough, a full tail of hair was there, too. The farmer scratched his head and murmured, "Strange things do be happening. You're eating your oats and your tails are back, and it wouldn't surprise me at all if my plowing was done."

Then back to the house he went. "Are you up yet?" he called to his wife.

"I am," she answered, "but it's a terrible strain I'm under. Somehow or other, the walnut slipped out from between me toes. And it's afraid I am to look at me bonnet."

"Sure, let me look at it for you," said he. "Strange things are happening."

He opened the hat box. "It's just as you left it, from the last county fair."

"Bring it to me," she called. "Sure I want to look at it anyway." She felt of the pewit's wing. "It's wet, it is," she said. "Tut, tut," said the farmer, "it's all in your mind."

The blind fiddler rubbed his blind eyes and called to his boy. "Wake up, you young rascal. The rooster is hoarse from crowing."

The boy got up and opened the door and stood looking away over the sea. He smiled to himself.

"They're back," he said.

"What do you be talking about?" the blind fiddler asked.

"Here's the lost bow to your fiddle, lying on the doorstep."

"Bring it to me!" cried the blind fiddler. "It's little I'm believing these days."

The blind fiddler felt of his bow. "Why, it is—it is. Now hand me my fiddle, till I finger a tune."

What he played was a strange weird tune that he'd never heard before. He laid the bow and fiddle down and jumped out of bed, saying:

"Is that a streak of daylight my blind eyes do be seeing?"

He made for the door and around the corner of the hut he ran.

"I say! I say!" he called to the boy. "That's the mist off the bog I see lifting!"

THE END

Coachwhip Publications

CoachwhipBooks.com

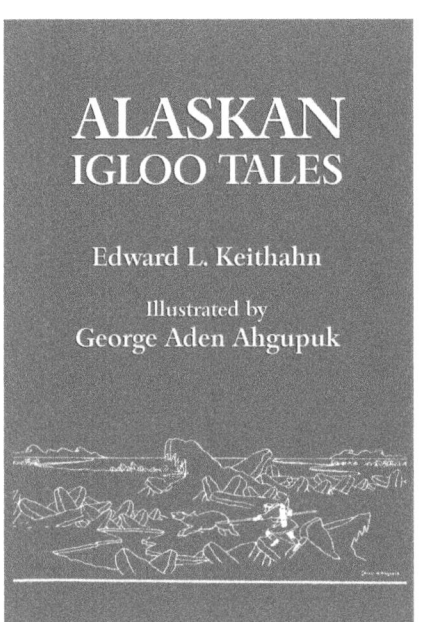

ALASKAN
IGLOO TALES

Edward L. Keithahn

Illustrated by
George Aden Ahgupuk

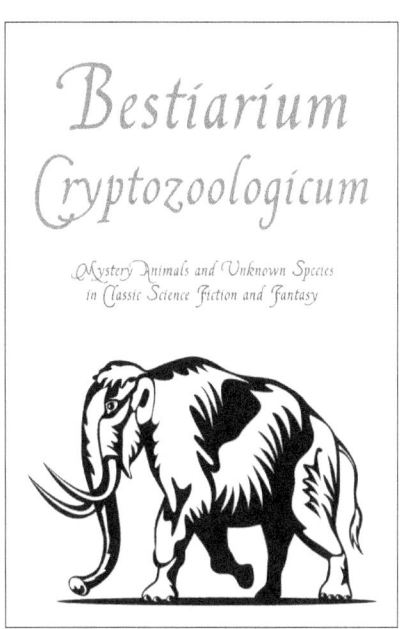

Bestiarium
Cryptozoologicum

Mystery Animals and Unknown Species
in Classic Science Fiction and Fantasy

THE LAST
MAMMOTH

Manly Wade
WELLMAN

The Adventures of
Darby O'Gill

and Other Tales
of Supernatural
Ireland

HERMINIE
TEMPLETON
KAVANAGH

Coachwhip Publications

CoachwhipBooks.com

THE CLAN OF MUNES
by
FREDERICK J. WAUGH

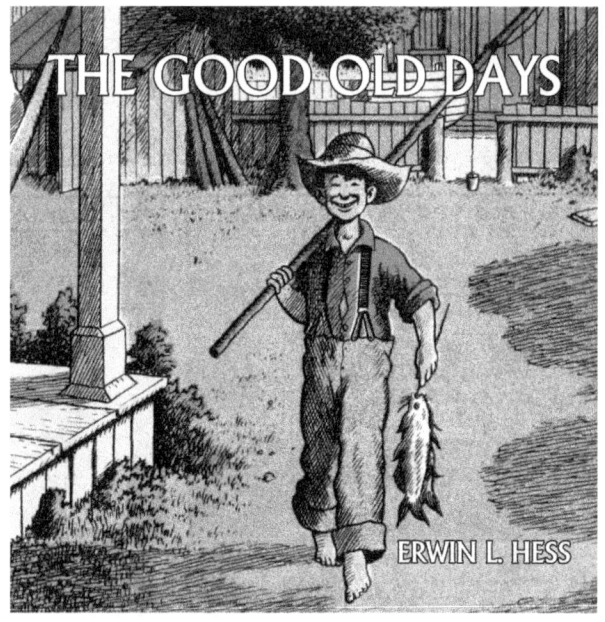

THE GOOD OLD DAYS

ERWIN L. HESS

Coachwhip Publications

CoachwhipBooks.com

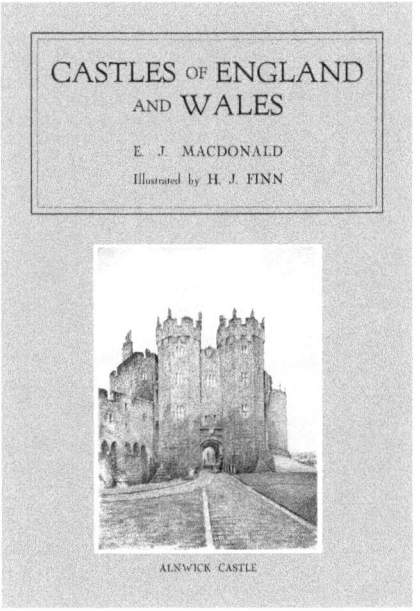

Coachwhip Publications

CoachwhipBooks.com

www.ingramcontent.com/pod-product-compliance
Lightning Source LLC
Chambersburg PA
CBHW071820020726
47502CB00004B/1177